MARDEN

PAYOFSKYI'S DISCOVERY

12.95

D1053494

Payofski's Dyscovery

Payofski's Dyscovery

———A NOVEL———

Hal Marden

INDIANA UNIVERSITY PRESS
BLOOMINGTON

Manufactured in the United States of America

Library of Congress Cataloging-in-Publication Data

Marden, Hal.
Payofski's dyscovery.

I. Title.
PS3563.A6438P3 1986   813'.54   85-45701
ISBN 0-253-34301-1

1   2   3   4   5   90 89 88 87 86

THE AUTHOR GRATEFULLY ACKNOWLEDGES
THE ASSISTANCE OF THE
THOMAS J. WATSON FOUNDATION

For dear Leanne
And dedicated to the memory of
Brad Simpson

Payofski's Dyscovery

Payofski's Dyscovery

Y ou are all you have. If Warren Paley meant anything by jumping that day in June, by killing himself, nobody I talked to later led me to believe he
meant anything else. If he had dived off the for-
tieth floor with the express purpose of landing on
Allston Weir it could be considered, cynically, a
nice effort and maybe the luckiest failure of his career. His foot just clipped
Allston on the shoulder, knocking him down on the street with the result
that Weir sat there, stunned and spattered with Paley's blood. And suddenly he was not himself. With the sound of shattering bone in his ears
he could not remember where he was, or who he was, or fathom the
meaning of the death of Paley, lying beside him in an impossible position.

An old woman who saw Warren hit ground turned her face to the
skyscraper and threw up on it. Mr. Weir, dazed, stockstill for a moment,
tried to stand up but his knees wobbled and he fell down again. His suit
was so blood-spattered the magazine vendor across the street took him
for the jumper and his jaw dropped in disbelief. A boy with a shaved head
and a bowie knife skated by the newsstand looking up, swearing in the
direction of the roof from which Paley had flown, arms thrown out, his
face turned up laughing at the sun.

The traffic began to bind up for a better look at the crowd and the
blood. Passersby jostled and formed a transfixed circle of faces staring
horrified at Mr. Weir. Looking up dismally, Allston Weir had blue eyes
pinched in shock. His suit was conspicuously tailored, light as a butterfly

on his broad shoulders and probably ruined. His shoes were Genoa leather polished to the same gleam as the gold in his wristwatch and his wedding band. Blood was everywhere. Simon Van Hyde, who had seniority at the Washington Street Shelter for Wayward Men, shambled at the edge of the circle looking for an opening, and when he found it he shouted, "Payofski!" and shoved the people aside. He flung his head this way and that. His hair flew in the people's faces. "Payofski! Can you stand? Let me help! When did you get back! Shit!" Van Hyde's gray hair flowed around a bald spot and over his sunglasses, which were missing the left lens. The right lens was mirrored. "Come on, Payofski!" he bellowed. "The police . . ." He tried to lift up the stunned man.

With his help Weir did stand but he jerked his arm away.

"Come on!" Van Hyde said. "This way! The police!" The people parted for them. "Where have you been? We've been waiting! Look at you! You found your uncle?" Van Hyde took him by the arm and out of the crowd and down the clogged street. The man followed blindly, wincing and touching his head. "Leave me alone," he said. "Don't touch me."

"Are you hurt? He landed almost on top of you! Just your luck, eh? Hasn't changed. My deepest sympathy!"

"Who are you?"

Van Hyde spread his dirty arms. "It's me! Simon! You're only gone a year and you forget? No!" he dropped his arms and wagged a finger. "You've been drinking, Payofski, here. Exhale. You can't hide it!"

He shoved Van Hyde's wretched face away. "Get away from me! I never heard of you!"

"Cossack! Two hundred proof," Van Hyde shook his head, obliging Payofski's confusion by walking behind. "It's all right! Deny it! You deny and I'll believe! Like the old days! Remember my bench? Here." He led him to a bench at the edge of the Public Garden. It faced away from the tragedy, toward the swanboats and rose beds. The man in pink followed as a concession to trying to remember, of all things, whether his name was Payofski or not. There seemed to be some obstacle—a block. But he sat where Van Hyde sat, and looked at the beech leaves and heard the sirens winding up far away as Van Hyde slapped the free space on the bench. "Everyone missed you! Sit closer. We were talking just the other day, Christopher and I. Christopher said, 'That Payofski! Probably found his uncle and got some money off him. Maybe a job!' And I said—forgive me," Van Hyde tugged at his rotten handkerchief, honked hoarsely into it and stuffed it back down as he broke wind. " 'He made up his uncle, I bet,' I said. 'He's a great talker, Payofski.' You—a shrewd man." He bent and slapped at the blood spots on the man's suit and the man shoved him away in exasperation.

"I got to you just in time!" Van Hyde bellowed, his lens scattering the sunlight, his free eye in mist. "If the police found you in these clothes they'd take you in for sure. Where'd you steal them?"

"Steal?" the sick man lowered his head. He was pale. "I don't have any idea what you're talking about or who you are. My name is not Payofski. Where am I? What happened?"

"Well you were walking down the street! I was about to yell to you when that man jumped! Almost on top of you!"

"Jumped . . . ," the man looked around. "Dead?"

"Yes. Bet his life on it!" Simon nodded vigorously. "These buildings grow another story every year, Payofski! These architects!" he threw up his hand. "Who will stop them? The higher they get, the higher they go! I was telling Christopher just the other . . ." The man in pink turned to stare back at the street. Police cruisers were arriving, their lights flashing. A police truck backed to the building and issued cadets who began to assemble a wooden cordon. One was wading into traffic with a whistle and the man scowled deeply. "What city is this?"

Van Hyde flung up his arm. "Boston! It's a town in Massachusetts, Payofski! Cradle of the Universe! Hub of liberty! A state of the U . . ."

"I know where Boston is," the man turned and saw himself in the mirrored lens. It was an abject sight. He had a boyish face with age lines radiating from his eyes. He looked as confused as he felt and felt twice as old as he looked.

"We've been through thick and thin!" Van Hyde bellowed at him. "Your uncle . . ."

"I'm sorry," the man said. "Forgive me. I never saw you before in my life. I don't know you. Please stop calling me Payofski."

"I see," said Van Hyde. "You did very well for yourself. And who are we this time, Payofski, Teilhard de Chardin? The Chancellor of Mexico?" He sat indignant.

"I don't know what right you have to insult me," the man said. He tried to stand but his knees gave way. He fell back to the bench shaking from nausea as Van Hyde stared and pitied him. It would always be the same for Payofski. Always struggling up out of the pit on a prayer, a lie, a stolen suit of clothes. "Another six inches and you would have been killed," Simon said.

"The police . . ."

"What about them?"

"I need to speak to them."

"Why—so they can take you out back and shoot you? They'll only ask where you got the suit. They'll tie you up by your thumbs and telephone every shop owner between here and Wilmington. Act sober." The vagrant sat closer, pontificating, his breath a garland of onion and vodka. "I and everyone else at the shelter will swear you've been out of town for a year. You'll know who your friends are then. The suicide did you a favor! Brought you back to your senses—your beginnings! Did us all a favor by snuffing his misery before he used it on us in some way. Fly away the miserable! Look, Payofski," he pointed into the Garden. "Christopher!" He waved him around. "Christopher, look who I found!"

A lumbering man seven feet tall with a cynical flat face and a beard and bloodshot eyes squinted their way. His arms were wrapped around a bag of chattering empty bottles. He wore a torn raincoat, holey unlaced boots and a smoking butt in his teeth. Shooting a look from Van Hyde to the mob uptown circulating around the dead man he boomed out a laugh, shook his Christ-like hair and said, "Another business gone bad!"

The man in pink looked up at this giant. He did not recognize him either. Christopher stood over the bench with a prejudicial squint and a beefy hand stuck out underneath the bottles. "Fuckin' Payofski!" Van Hyde lifted his shoulders to Payofski as if to say, You see?

"He says he's not Payofski, Christopher. He says he wants to go to the *police*."

"Ho, I'll take you to the police. How's your uncle, you slime? What happened to my share? You spend it? I wouldn't want to be you if I was you either."

"There's been a mistake. I was hit on the head," said the man, "and . . ." He looked suddenly surprised and whispered, "My wallet," and began patting the suit. "I can't remember . . . if I could find . . ."

Van Hyde winked at Chris, ejecting his thumb above his mouth and said, "Vodka," doccing his tongue.

However much they got a kick out of Payofski trying to be somebody, they obliged him and led him to the police. Headquarters was a granite mausoleum with vaulted ceilings that rounded the echoes and harbored the sun. Christopher sat on a railway bench, put his bottles down and chose a butt from the sand pedestal. He scraped his wood match on his zipper and bared his teeth at a secretary passing Castilian-heeled, popping her gum, leaving him in a cloud of perfume. Van Hyde led Payofski to the sergeant of the day, one Leon Carey, who listened with disdain as the bloodstained man in pink said, "I was walking down the street when a man killed himself. I think he must have hit me on the head, and I can't remember anything. I have . . . anemia."

"What's your name?" Carey asked.

"No, no, you don't understand."

"Payofski," said Van Hyde, his greasy fingers at the edge of the desk. Sergeant Carey looked down between him and the confused man at his side; then wiggling his fingers at the sick man, he said, "Identification."

"I don't *have* any!"

"So where are you from? What kind of work do you do? Come on, out with it, I knock off in five minutes."

"Payofski" shook his head. It was like a bad dream. "If I could remember anything," he said, "anything at all, including what I'm doing here, I wouldn't be here!"

"His name is *Payofski*, your honor. From the Washington Street Shelter for Wayward *Men*, a facility of the American Red *Cross*. He left a year ago to find his *uncle*, a world-famous pornographical novelist, who he said owed him some *money*. Which money he was going to *share*," Van Hyde stared hard at Payofski.

Sergeant Carey looked from one to the other and back again. "How," he lifted his pencil, "can he know you, and you not know him?"

"If I could tell you that, I would be on my way home, or to my doctor, or wherever I was going when the man was killed." He stepped forward. "The body hit me on the head!"

Carey hunched his shoulders and leaned forward. "So what do you want me to do? This man knows you. Seems to me you ought to believe him. If you think someone might be interested in who you are or where you are, I'll take your prints. I can put you down as missing."

"Missing."

"Missing. But you won't officially be missing anywhere for forty-eight hours. How's that?"

"It'll do," Payofski, not yet resigned to being, drummed his fingers and looked aside in thought. Missing—fingerprints. "Reasonable," he said, nodding, turning back to the desk and the practical sergeant. "There's one other thing I would like to ask you, one man to another. A favor."

Carey ducked low, his chin near the desk surface. Payofski moved close.

"I have no money."

It was significant that he whispered. But he was not keen enough to his thoughts or manners that choosing to plead impecuniousness to a cop told Weir anything about who he was. It was not Sergeant Carey's or the department's responsibility, but Leon Carey lent ten dollars of his own, thinking he would never see it again. No matter—the lost man was finger-printed. His pictures were taken because it was reasonable. Because it was reasonable—because it was not reasonable to doubt the word of two men with memories against the word of one without, and because the men of the Washington Street Shelter were visited regularly by a doctor, he went the way of Van Hyde and the giant, hesitating but following anyway. He walked along, head bent, searching for memories that disappeared as they began, all sparks from a fire. The harder he tried to recall himself the more it was like searching for something in the dark with someone else's hand. The frustration of seeing himself in the glass of the city, his face in the windows and against advertisements, was almost worse than arriving at the shelter. But not quite.

It was suppertime on Washington Street. A rabble of men was lined up at a locked black door waiting for food. When they saw the amnesiac some of them yelled, "Payofski! Payofski's back! Payofski, you scum!" and other terms of affection. They were rejects, alcoholics and misfits, dusky old men who pawed his shoulders, grinned through loose teeth, hawked spit on the linoleum and cursed, gawking at the pink suit and gold watch worth ten times the furniture in the room. At one time the building was a Swedenborgian church. Now it was a nest of failed humanity with a narthex that reeked of fatback and urea. It was an asylum overseen by a man with baggy eyes, tired clothes and the smile of a saint who opened the black door, and Van Hyde signaled Payofski to step in line ahead of him, which he did, to shuffle along with the rest and wonder what he had done to deserve this. What but out of a sense of despair, in the face of disgust for the broccoli soup ladled by a girl named Jane, or to charity in general, he didn't know about himself might come yet in private feelings. He got caught up in the shuffling line and the pace annoyed him. He watched the men paw bread out of a steel basin and take the chipped plastic bowls from the girl with a reverential nod and shaking hands. He noticed that some of the men closed their eyes when the soup was handed over.

He followed Van Hyde to a long table near the wall, and there the shame settled on him. Gradually men opened their eyes and looked. Payofski's uncle came up in some slurred question of fame and when one of the men spat bread in the question, "Where'd you get the ring?" the others looked down. Leadenness prevented the man from speaking. He hadn't noticed—a band of diamond-studded gold as thick as a cable around his finger.

"You married, Payofski?" someone asked. Payofski turned his hand over. The ring dazzled them and Payofski frowned. To him, Payofski or not, this church of failure was populated by men who sensed the dream life offered in wherever he had acquired the suit and the ring. Without knowing who he was therefore a clue was provided. They stared at him and his jewelry and slurped the soup as one of them named Richfield, drunk and facetious, challenged him to say how much of this his pornographic uncle had contributed. Just enough, thought the man, that all he could feel for Richfield and the others was an alloy of sorrow and contempt, and from that to feel he must not be Payofski at all.

When they finished supper a group of men drifted out to the courtyard to plot how to escape themselves in drink. Others picked their teeth and fell on the cots, pulling the blankets over their faces to dream. Not "Payofski." He sat on what Van Hyde said was Payofski's cot and took off his jacket and searched the pockets. Anything would help. He turned the jacket around and inside out; he was a sturdily built man in good condition. His gut was trim. His eyes, unlike the pickled gazes of these men, were sky blue and expressive. He looked like a man who had contracted middle age with grace, as if he had asked it to dance, and though he never stepped on its toes, he never let it lead either. Ten minutes' searching revealed nothing but this impression of cool vanity, five keys on a silver ring, and in the breast pocket of his jacket a black and white photograph of a mountain. The keys only teased him. In the photograph a girl of eleven or twelve stood holding the forestay of an iceboat. Nothing was written on the back, but Payofski held this photo in his hands like a missal, certain that seconds before the accident he had known everything about it. Known everything about the locks the ring of keys opened. Everything about the ring. Everything about the pink suit and the man inside it. Even finding a cigar and unpersonalized handkerchief was finding objects mute as the dead: Only the picture and ring could lead him from amnesia back into the stream of his life.

He was thinking it over when a man in the corner wrenched himself free of the garbage cans and stumbled across the floor. It was Mr. Richfield. In his former life a professor of Russian literature, Richfield looked like a boxer taking short steps, whirling burly with big ears and a sunburnt neck, stormy eyes and an ashen face. He wore a T-shirt with academic insignia on the right breast and a dirty red stripe that formed a line when he flung a paperback against the wall over Payofski's cot. The book splatted down and Payofski jumped. Richfield drew himself up and hauled at his trousers and pointed, his finger stabbing the air. "*You* ain't Payofski!" he screamed. "You're an impostor! A fake! Who are you! Who are you!"

In the seventy-two hours that followed Payofski found himself the object of friendships, enmity and greed. If he was Payofski, if he was not Payofski, he was someone who owed money and who had money owed to him. He was a man who had betrayed men and who had been betrayed. He had sued for ownership of nonessentials with his fists and avenged friends and been avenged. The more he learned as Payofski, the harder he tried to live up to the arrangements the wayward men imposed on him as Payofski, ever believing that one Mr. Payofski was having his life changed in proxy by the wiles of a man in a pink suit with amnesia. This man referred Payofski's creditors to his debtors and vice versa, retracted accusations he had never made, backed down from fistfights he wasn't stupid enough to have picked, consoled the men Payofski had wounded and vowed restitution to those Payofski had cheated—all without feeling a moiety of shame or attachment.

He was resourceful, whoever he was. If the police he visited every day were saturnine or careless he at least had the snapshot of the mountain for comfort. When Sergeant Carey told him that based on a check of fingerprints he had never been in trouble with the law, he asked Carey, "Tell me—did Payofski?" The answer was somehow no. Feeling blue, he returned to the shelter, sat on his cot and put his chin in his hand to think. This was how Christopher found him—Christopher with the bulk and extortionary scowl, the dirty beard and torn trousers, the change of redeemed bottles jingling in his pocket. "You really think you ain't Payofski?"

The man looked up at him. If he was Payofski he did not remember that he was, or if he was then he valued the amnesia and wanted to keep it. He was in a state. Christopher, unanswered, turned away and said, "So you're too smart for Payofski." And when he had half crossed the room he stopped. He turned around again and glowered, "You better hope, anyway. I always gave you the benefit of the doubt, Payofski. If you're lying this time I think I could kill you."

When Friday came around the man who operated the shelter converted a classroom into an examining room for the doctor. The day he arrived he was Payofski's last hope. Maurice Topsenfeld, M.D., included the shelter on his rounds of bringing succor to the people he thought needed it most—poor people. Dr. Topsenfeld comforted indigents like the wayward men, addicts, bums and the dispossessed he turned up in hovels and rainy holes in the city, cowering like insects in some rock-hard stale cake. Topsenfeld was simian with fat hands and oily black hair, a perennially unkempt man with soiled ties and white shirts stained yellow at the collar. Some men may be born never to comb their hair or concentrate on their outward selves; if so Topsenfeld was such a man. He shouldered his seedy jackets into dangerous parts of the city, aware of eyes trained on him through broken glass and the washing hung out in the fog like the hair of Medusa. He plied, the good doctor, past gushing hydrants and wrecked cars, his black bag like a shield beaten dull. The sick waited— people whose flu was drug withdrawal, whose self-defeat was largely the lack of honest work to do. Maurice Topsenfeld went to them smoking like a chimney, and with a .357 magnum on his belt that Friday he opened the bag in the Swedenborgian classroom and produced a piece of paper from which he read, "Mr. Payofski?" And he stared at the gentleman before him, stripped to his underwear, muscular—handsome in a sort of corporate American way, who slammed his fist down on the tissue-swathed table and shouted, "My name is not Payofski!"

"Right," said Maurice, and extracting his stethoscope he palpated Payofski's chest. "Deep breath."

"I was walking down the street. And I got hit on the head. I can't remember a thing."

"Again."

"You have to understand. I can't recall my name or where I came from. I have a picture of a mountain. Please," he took it out of his pants. "It *means* something to me. Look. It exists. Does that make sense? I can almost remember it. Please look. I don't belong in this shelter, is all I can tell you. I need your help. *I am not Payofski!*"

"Cough."

"Damnit, man! *Listen* to me!"

"No," Dr. Topsenfeld snapped the stethoscope from his ears. "I know you're not Mr. Payofski. The likeness is, however, remarkable." He lifted a clipboard, and it bounced in his hand as he made notes. "Mr. Payofski is dead," he put in, scratching his nose with the pen.

"Thank God."

"Murdered. A year ago, by his uncle."

"My condolences." Weir fell back on the table. And as Dr. Topsenfeld noted his hygiene and apparently good health, the fitness of his skin and tone of his muscles, the man who was not Payofski stepped off the table and pulled on his sleeve.

"You'll need an electroencephalogram," he said. "And X rays. You'll want blood and a CT to rule out . . ."

With a raised hand Dr. Topsenfeld stopped him. From the folding chair by the blackboard he spoke.

"If you were Payofski," he said, "you would be dirty, incoherent, drunk, begging me for narcotics, incomprehensibly foul-mouthed and robbing me blind. As it is you have foresight, you know the names of some medical tests for neurological damage, though you don't know your own name," he put up his hand again. "Don't worry, I believe you. You're well-mannered, sober, articulate, and unless I'm mistaken, you're afraid. But who, I'm forced to remind you, is going to pay for all this?"

"Damnit, man!" the stranger brought up in his clenched fist a banner of the tissue and shook it. "Five days ago I could have told you who I was like it was nothing! I could have introduced you to my wife—do you see this ring? Do you know what this ring must have cost? Some lunatic dived off a skyscraper and landed on me! Now I'm living in church with a bunch of misfits who say I owe them everything from their lives to the moon! Meanwhile my life is on hold somewhere while you ask me who has the cash that'll let me pick up where I left off! Now you tell me, Dr. Topsenfeld, what the hell a man is supposed to do about that!"

Dr. Topsenfeld composed himself. He looked at the raging man not Payofski and snapped flame to a cigarette with a chrome lighter. Through the curtain of smoke he exhaled he said, "Let me see," and dropped the lighter back in his pocket, "your ring again."

It opened doors, that ring. It was a monster. For its weight in diamonds and gold came some of the greatest tortures of modern medicine; for a cup of Weir's urine, a bag of his blood, a sample of stool and a drop of semen came a darkened room with a machine that whirled around his brain, knee bends with a vial exploded under his nose as his heart hammered and his penis flogged his ankles. All particulars were registered and counted by a blond nurse who called him Mr. Doe and marched him from room to room with Nazi efficiency.

They put his blood in a centrifuge and spun it. They magnified the teeming cells of his dung 10,000 times. Every weapon of medicine available for the pledge of a wedding ring was applied to discovering who he was.

They pipetted his marrow and laying him on his side, they tapped vital fluids he did not even know existed. He bent over a chair and a grizzled oriental doctor with a beard pulled on a surgical finger and slid it inside his rectum. "Forgive, please," said the oriental man, and with the end of his finger he wrung the anonymous prostate till the anonymous penis wept. The anonymous man bit his lip and hung on. He hung on for two days. For two days he was poked, prodded and needled, stabbed, sucked, burned, bled and aerated, consoled, warned, cauterized, told to run now stop, put to sleep and brought to, laid back and with his cock lifted he felt the slide of a coiled wire swab into the end. All of this thanks to the fortune of having married some woman he could not remember.

When he left the hospital for headquarters at the end of the second day it was with a limp and a repudiation of the art as well as the science of medicine. If Sergeant Carey seemed to be a louse, he was at least by now an interested one. Because Payofski had repaid the ten dollars Carey had taken to him and expected his daily arrival in the pink suit and unlaundered shirt. The sergeant shared his disappointment that in each day's missing persons report there was no description even remotely resembling him. He also noticed that Payofski's appearance was changing every day, as if the act of discovering oneself were subject to the laws of decay. It was as if, if things went any further, the stranger could never be found because he could not possibly be missed. The man he was, was gone; the man he was going to be was not formed yet.

He may not have been sick before the tests, but he felt sick after. He stood at the sink in the men's room of the Washington Street Shelter, his pale ass hung out as he scrubbed his undershirt and briefs. As he passed through the sleeping room the men fell silent out of respect for him. When he fell on Payofski's cot some men staggered past and slurred expressions of sympathy and encouragement. Some offered him swigs from hidden bottles to show they trusted him. One walked by and whispered, "Payofski, good luck! Good luck!" and he said, "Payofski's dead, you idiot." Others thought he was going batty in the wrong direction—toward the terrors of self-sufficiency. Mr. Richfield, the once professor, incensed by the airs Payofski put on, clambered out of the ashcans sputtering high German, his gray face lean like a hawk's, his eyes scathing and upper lip curled under. He flung a newspaper at the wall above the cot, and with the personals in his fist pointed his finger and said, "You're a coward! You are not free! You have nothing! You are nothing! You are the prisoner of a delusion! You wish to be someone else, but you are stuck! There is no way out! You are a failure! You are a failure! You are a failure!"

The stranger closed his eyes, lifted his arm, and flipped his middle finger into a small pole.

"You *are* Payofski!" Richfield yelled. "You *are* Payofski! You *are!*"

All the wayward men cheered. At each refrain Richfield stabbed his finger and shook the paper. They yelled the name Payofski and waited for him to give in—to drop this idea of being a man with something more than a little shaving kit bought with Sergeant Carey's ten bucks and credit at the hospital. Richfield whirled, opened the crumpled paper, and turned to the others.

"But Mr. Payofski has run an *advertisement* in the dailies! Here's his picture on page five!" He held it up. "It says, 'Anyone with information about the identity of this man should contact Area D police headquarters. Ask for Sergeant Carey'! Oh?? Shall we contact headquarters, gentlemen?"

The men cheered again. They laughed and derided Payofski, but once Richfield fell asleep they filed past and whispered, "Good luck, Payofski! Good luck!" He really believed he had a place in the world. When they next looked for him the cot was empty.

Five blocks away, by the wharfs, he rounded the corner, his head down, his hands behind his back. "Ah," he said, nodding, staring at the pavement. Beside him Maurice Topsenfeld wheezed as he walked, swinging the battered bag, his hand still fragrant with the iron and blood of a newborn baby. Maurice liked the smells of birth. "So you see the amnesia was just a symptom," he said. "The disease is called gyracinguloplasticchoreosis. It's a lesion on a body of your brain called the hippocampus."

Payofski bowed his head and listened. Topsenfeld looked straight ahead to give his patient the option of looking afraid if he wished. The sun burned crimson on the harbor and gulls lighted on the roofs.

"To what do I owe this gyra . . . ?" asked the man.

"Unknown. There's some literature on it—not much. And the treatment is theoretical," the doctor lit a small cigar. It was a boy. A cloud passed by the sun and darkened them. "At least you're not Payofski?" he chuckled.

"No. Thank you. Cingulo—?"

"Gyracinguloplasticchoreosis."

"Enough name there for the three of us."

Dr. Topsenfeld laughed politely. He looked up and asked, "Any luck with the newspaper?"

"Not yet."

"Can I take you somewhere? You could stay with me. In my room I have a Murphy . . ."

"Thanks, no," he turned, "really." The wind blew his hair. The ships docked along the pier looked rusted to the earth. The two men shook hands in the wind and when the stranger laughed, Dr. Topsenfeld laughed. Both men laughed, the fat doctor wiping tears from his eyes, the stranger with the gyracinguloplasticchoreosis laughing with his forehead in his hand.

Two days later he was standing in line for his food when the telephone in the baggy-eyed man's little office rang, and the baggy-eyed man stuck out his head and said, "Payofski! Sergeant Carey at Area D!"

All talk ceased. The line shuffled to a halt. Jane stood transfixed at the end of her ladle. The pigeons in the courtyard buckled and exploded on high and in Mr. Richfield's eyes was murder.

"Some woman down there to claim you. Says she's your wife!" He slammed the door.

The men stared. Somehow he had done it—magicked himself into another chance. If he had a wife then he must have a civilized place for his wife to live (wives insisted). He must have plumbing and a dentist. He looked around. Subdued and guilty that failure had failed to hold him, some of the men could not look at him. A faint smile started across his face, his sickness notwithstanding. The men broke the line, hovered around him and clapped his back and shoulders. They shook his hand. Payofski—

whoever—felt inflated with goodwill. His heart pounded. His life had not neglected him.

For the first and last time he sat down with the wayward men and ate with appetite—the soyloaf, boiled beans and sour lettuce. The air was haunted by murmurs of triumph. "Payofski!" they said. "Fuckin' Payofski!"—a name he acknowledged now as a step surpassed. He deposited his plate and spoon in the tray and sneaked off to shave. It was a day too filled with relief and approbation to think about the cut or character of a woman who claimed to be his wife. Sunlight streamed into the courtyard where five men stood under the glittery leaves, the salt breeze roiling over the stone wall, and got it in their minds that Payofski's miracle must be theirs too by association. They had helped. Owing to the egalitarian quality of misery they were sure Payofski would take them, and so they packed what they had. They shuffled around Payofski's cot like old, improbable planets around an improbable sun. He was somebody. Payofski would lead. Perhaps they all had wives, and jobs with an eternity of vacation time, liquor cabinets, savings accounts and beachfront property. They shuffled and stared at the clock. Suddenly Van Hyde shoved his way in, flinging his hair in their faces and yelling, "Break it up! Break it up!" waving his arms, pushing them away, accusing them of bad manners. He turned with a mirrored grin to his friend.

"I will escort you to the police station," he said, "Mr. Whomever."

"Good luck!" said the men. "Good luck! Break a leg! Call when you get there, Payofski!"

"Collect, Payofski!"

Towering over the rabble Christopher eyed the man in the reddish brown suit as if he were a hero. Even Richfield, on the ceremony of Payofski's last urination in the Washington Street Shelter for Wayward Men, offered up the paper towels and whispered that he would like a job if there was an opening. Or barring that maybe the stranger would find himself well off enough that he would come back at the holidays with a television set and some eggnog. "I can do anything," Mr. Richfield said. The stranger thanked him and went out to the courtyard. A starling preened in the beech tree. The leaves glittered in the late sun shining on a world he belonged to. With Simon Van Hyde's mirrored eye a beacon, the man not Payofski took a deep breath, patted his empty pockets out of habit, and set out to recover himself.

[14] *Payofski's Dyscovery*

Hatching Hector's Plot

My name is Foster Ames, by the way, Allston Weir's doctor and friend. If there were laws against taking advantage of a man with a sick memory then you might blame the men of the shelter as I have, at times, for misguiding a man who was not who they thought he was. But excuse them as victims of their own delusion and put the blame on the ones who intentionally led him to believe he was someone else. The following scheme was Hector Paley's idea, I know that for a fact now, even if its sinister elegance appealed to Julie Weir Paley at the time, and for certain ulterior reasons of her own, she agreed to do it . . . .

When Simon Van Hyde led Allston into Area D headquarters that day, Sergeant Carey smiled and said, "A woman named Mrs. Warren Paley," and he turned over a release form. "372 B Street, here for you." Allston looked around. "She says you're sick, Mr. Paley. Like I didn't know. Anyway that's your name, can you remember that? Me, I'm sick of you. Sign here, Paley, God love you."

"Where?" he asked, meaning not the whereabouts of the dotted line but those of the woman, his wife. The only woman in sight was the secretary with the fuck-me blue heels and nasty sashay. "What woman?"

He turned in time to catch her coming out of the phone booth. The door sprang in and Julie leaped up and threw her arms around his neck. She was crying . . . the sick man struggled to breathe; he had not seen her face. He could make out a shoulder, a wave of black hair, her figure plumbed over her shoulder, cased the length of her back. She was almost strangling him. "Shhhhhhhhh," he said, patting her and trying to pry her off as he whispered consoling words. She was slender and very strong. Her hair was lush, hot and perfumed. He was drowning in it. She seemed to be wearing a black leotard and cotton madras skirt to the ankles and flat shoes. All this she rubbed against him until he could pull her away, and he found she was, for what he took to be his wife, very young.

"Hello," he said. "Thank you for coming."

"God," she said, holding her head exactly as he had when Maurice gave him the diagnosis.

"I'll explain everything," he said, searching her eyes. If she was a day older than twenty-two he was Napoleon. She was strikingly more beautiful than he ever hoped.

"Sign," said Carey.

"Julie?"

"Sign."

"Of course," he took the pen nervously. "I am . . . ?"

"Paley. Warren."

"L-Y?"

"L-E-Y."

He looked at her. He remembered—slightly. The sensation of a cat brushing his leg in the dark was how the memory came. It seemed she had been crying for days. Her hand shook and she lay her head on his chest as he held her and signed. That thin mouth, those eyes—he seemed to be, Warren Paley, a man of taste.

"I remember you," he whispered. "It's all right." All this Van Hyde observed from a distance.

"This release here says this is your wife and the Boston Police helped you locate her to your satisfaction, etc. Mrs. Paley thank you for coming by. You're a lovely woman." She looked up quietly, brushing a tear away. Simon Van Hyde frowned.

"Have you seen a doctor?" she said in a clogged voice.

"Yes. I traded my ring."

"Your . . . " She held his hand up. She kissed his ring finger. "You remember me?"

"I think," he said. "Yes, something . . . maybe not everything. We'll talk. I'm sorry. It's—you're—on the tip of my tongue."

Skeptical that Payofski was grasping at his true life in this girl's arms, Van Hyde shook his head since to his specular left eye and bloodshot, naked right one, the girl looked like trouble. She was dark; perhaps, he thought, she was a witch. As she left headquarters with the ghost of Payofski, Van Hyde raised his hand. He wanted to say something oracular. It was too late—she was stepping into a cab. He with his shaving bag and soiled suit stepped in behind and sat beside her. She held his hand on her knee. The meter flag dropped and they were off. In the cab Julie stared and brushed styptic from his cheek. "Did you make an appointment at the hospital?"

"You know about the cingulo . . . "

She pronounced it for him. "You must have been terrified," she said. "I didn't know where you went."

"No," he looked away, then down. "My clothes . . . "

She hugged his arm and laughed and cried. The cab tore around the city, horn blaring, the driver running the lights and cursing America in Sicilian. The sun was low now; the fiery blood of dusk layered the ocean and tinged Julie's skin scarlet and passion blue. She was shaking.

"How long have I had this illness?"

"A long time," she said. "Years and years."

The driver took a deep corner that forced him against her and he apologized. "This driver seems insane. Things happen so fast here. And so slow."

She looked away.

"A man jumped off a building and killed himself. Or someone pushed him. It's been chaos. I don't mean to upset you." He drew her head to his chest. The gesture seemed familiar. "The next thing I knew a vagrant was convinced I was Payofski."

"Payofski?"

"Yes. Is this the face of an Armenian?"

"You mean Pole, I think," she said softly. "Maybe, since you shaved your beard. You haven't been clean-shaven since . . . I can't remember. You look so young."

"Paley is Polish?" he looked out the window. "I must sound like a fool."

Julie looked away too. The cab was barreling down a narrow industrial street. Sunlight slanted down five-story warehouses and fire escapes and the shadows were long. Payofski no longer, he watched the buildings unfold like a diorama of his life. If Julie had spoken the truth then she'd have said, "Our lives are a mess, and our marriages bad." But she watched him secretly, praying, her thoughts racing as fast as the hack before he braked and got his money. She said nothing to him, and when the cab tore away he followed her into a building that fifty years ago had been a winery. She led him up three dim flights of stairs, and behind her he eyed the figure she cut, and thought thoughts not becoming a man who had been her husband for five years.

She turned her key in the door and opened the apartment to him. This was not his home, but though he might have anticipated something different, something in grass, say, he could have fallen down and kissed it. Vestige of Payofski, he tried not to act overwhelmed. It was no palace. The space was divided into rooms by wallboard on studs that didn't reach the ceiling. The hall led to a living area Julie presented to him in silence— a mix of practical, staid furniture with an old fireplace. The pictures on the mantel brought him up short. He looked at them and picked them up carefully. There he was—a picture of him with her. His arm was around her. She looked unconscionably young. Every picture seemed an affidavit or proof that he was not Payofski and never had been, and he was grateful. The sunlight came down through a dusty skylight and two grimy windows and he found her staring at some spot on the floor.

"I could tattoo my name in my palm," he said.

"I'll show you around." She seemed embarrassed.

The bedroom had three high windows and a bureau. He assumed they shared it, and there was their bed. "It's not very comfortable."

"It looks wonderful, compared to Payofski's cot."

She led him through the back hall by the bathroom with a capacious tub on claw feet, and the kitchen where she went to another sashed window and pointed down at the alley and a little garden. "Celery, tomatoes, and chives." She turned, her hands folded. "Please," she said, "sit down." He sat—at a maple refectory table that he could not remember buying although he had. He watched her and basked in sentiments. I could put my hands around her waist, maybe, and touch fingertips. But not so fast. What a figure she had, and that childlike face. When she passed the window he understood by silhouette why he had traded bachelorhood for marriage if that was ever an issue: She wore no slip. The desire he felt for her that first day was the desire a man felt for a strange woman— desire for conquest rather than reunion. He did not suspect her, certainly not of complicity in any scheme to humiliate him, and he did not stare too long but looked at the garden, craning his neck as she chopped vegetables, and before long they were simmering on the stove—celery, chives, and tomatoes. He breathed it all in. He looked at the plates on hooks on the wall, a wine bottle with dried flowers on a breadbox and memos on a cork board. Home again. The silence reminded him of the confusion of the shelter, and Julie said, as if she had read his thoughts, "It will all come back to you soon. It always does." He glanced at her. She seemed to regret this.

The gumbo she made was terrible. He took the steaming plate from her with his eyes closed and dipped his fork in. Weary of viewing his life through the warped lens of an accident, he looked at the food and at Julie and it was not only palatable, everything, it was good. It was his. Stomach it, he thought—forget what's passed (that was easy). Drink in the sanity. He sat straight in the dirty suit at the broken-leafed table and tapped the pepper shaker. His feet together in the scuffed shoes, he had a thousand questions. He asked all he could get in and ate like a starving man. How old are you, and how old am I? Where were we married and for what reason? What is this address? Are we happy? Do we have friends—enemies? Children? When he realized he was bombarding her he stopped. Julie looked off and blushed. Something was wrong, he felt, something . . . Who was she?

"If I've had this cingulo-whatever all these years," he folded his hands, "I must have a doctor."

"You did. But he was a bastard. I fired him."

"Oh, good. Thanks."

She ate only one helping of vegetables. The anxiety of thinking his life could vanish faster than he had been returned to it might have changed him. He did not want to feel unconfident, to act uncertain, yet . . . perhaps she was this reserved all the time? He was not used to women with secrets. He was not used to women at all, he realized, when she stood up and dumped her plate in the sink and wiped her hands on a towel. The sun was going down in the garden, a deep, moving violet light. She said, "I have to get ready for work," and walked out.

"Wait . . . ," he said, hand up. His work. Where did he get his money? He stood and walked down the back hall and stood outside the bedroom, hesitating.

"One more thing—Julie?" he said. "My work? What am I?"

A drawer closed. He heard an atomizer spray and the rustle of her skirt.

"Down the hall, the room with the closed door . . . . "

Ah, an office at home. That was for the best. He walked down the hall to the indicated door and opened it. It looked as if a bomb had gone off in that room. It looked like the scene of some crime, trashing, vandalism—he couldn't be sure. An office in the traditional sense it was not. He strode in, his hands in his pockets. Against the four walls was a collection of paintings. The light of the dying sun poured through a dusty window and a skylight in the ceiling. Canvases stood on easels and hung from wires. The smell of paint and turpentine settled around him. There was barely a place to walk, the floor was a strew of canvas—rolls of it— and sketchpads, library books, and against the wall a scoliotic sofa riddled with cigarette burns. Oil paints and tubes of acrylic, a big incandescent palette made a confused mess of some shelves on the far wall. Fan brushes and knives were thrown around as if someone had left in a hurry. He stood there, entranced and confused.

Then a sort of smile played over his face. Told that all this was his, he believed; tripping on a roll of canvas, he wound up sitting on the floor and staring. The cat of recollection brushed his leg again. The colors of the paintings were bold—the reds of old wine and blood, sunsets, the yellows of jaundice and sunlight, the blues of the sea and dry ice. Landscapes, urban scapes in brown and gray and the surfaces of city water iridescent with the light of traffic and oil. They were works of vision, and he was humbled to think that if that . . . despite gyraplastic . . . portraits— the faces! They spoke to him. The paintings spoke his name like orphans trapped here by his disease, and here he was again, freeing them.

The grief Julie felt standing behind him in the doorway was unspeakable. She had shucked the skirt for jeans; her lush hair was bound in a ponytail and shoved up in a blue beret. When he sensed her there, he turned and spread his arms with a frown.

"I paint?"

She looked at him.

"An artist," he said absently.

"I have to go."

His knees cracked as he stood up.

"I have to go. I'll be back at three."

"But tell me where."

"The Fort Point Frame Shop," she said. "I frame pictures. We need the money." She left. The front door slammed. He heard her running down the hollow stairs and when he tripped back through the canvases and frames and easels and stumbled to the murky window, he saw her running down the street, her hand on her beret, the street long and dark and quiet like a tunnel.

The lesion had marooned Allston for nine days without his name, his wife, his career, his past, and his future. Now that he had an identity again he was left to find out who he was and what he was made of, and though he suspected he had done something to cause his wife to lose faith in him, he knew he would have to wait for her to remind him of what.

I was of course the doctor she had "fired." For twenty years I had been Ally's doctor. I was his friend for ten before that. He was a man of resources and energy. He was not a man to wear pink suits in deference to fashion. That ruined suit was the most expensive suit he owned, and when he took it off it was not his fault that all he knew was that he was a painter named Warren Paley. He did not remember that for five years as Julie's husband, Warren Paley had shored up their marriage with dreams of glory, fortune, wealth and artistic privilege. The truth was he was no more successful an artist than the rabble he had escaped downtown, and before he forgot everything he knew, he had been a hell of a lot unhappier. Oh, he had recollections of painting—knowledge of art, a private technique. He was a good painter. But Julie did not hesitate to remind him that in his career, such as it was, he had sold only two works—a watercolor of Olmsted Park during a flood and an oil of a pregnant woman holding an elliptical hula-hoop, entitled *The Eclipse of Sonja*.

That night he went to the bedroom and shucked the pink suit for the clothes he found in the closet—paint-stained shirts a size too big, bleached, ten years old, and cotton pants with drawstrings that billowed around the ankles, a size too big. "I'll love her better than before," he thought, turning to look at himself in the mirror, finding the image—a bohemian without a beard—"appropriate." He was a man eager to be at what he was, after the shelter, to be whatever it took.

That night he stood in the shabby clothes at the threshold of his life. With the works spread before him, he had to admit that he had forgotten the inspirations. Some made absolutely no sense to him. But if he would recover his continuity he knew he must be methodical, and he sucked back a sigh and waded into the rubble of sketches, oils and scenes of deep woods, city buildings and angels. He found a pencil and paper on the chaotic shelves and began to rearrange. In the skylight there was a moon and in the window stars and he began. The war scenes would go here and landscapes there. One must take stock, if there has been a lapse. Categorize and memorize; wake up. Portraits here, paintings of social commentary here. The abstracts and the nudes—the nudes! He took a break with the nudes. When he came across a nude of his beautiful Julie he sat down crosslegged. His heart banged his ribs like a caged monkey. He shook his head and thumbed the sweat from his eyes. It was an oil portraying her on the sofa, her arm extended to the floor with a crumb she offered to a fieldmouse. The painting looked so accomplished and beyond his means now, he put it where he could see it. For six hours he moved canvases and frames, discovered the images that formed his inner life, organized his colors and brushes, clearing the floor inch by inch. He tore the studio down and resurrected it, planting every picture in his memory like a seed. A man his age had no time to waste. Impatience drove him. He was a man of affairs—a janitor of his soul that night, sower of false memories and organizer of his failures. At three when Julie came home, her work smock bundled under her arm, she found the studio looking like a museum, the paintings arranged, the brushes soaking in glasses of clear water, issues of *Artifact* piled neatly in the closet, the palettes arrayed on the wooden shelf, the floor swept and the window polished, the skylight scared of gulls, the easels set up as accurately to the light as Stonehenge. She stepped into the room as if it were haunted. In the middle of the floor he slept with a bucket of dirty water by his head. There was a stack of paintings he had rejected as worthless and a stack he accepted as good, worth the effort, worth money. She looked at all this as if it were a miracle.

His eyes fluttered open. He pulled himself into a sitting position. "Julie . . . ?" She jumped and put her hand to her chest. "That painting," he pointed at a portrait of her. "You have a black eye in that painting. Why did I paint you with a black eye?"

She moved no closer and no farther away. "It's called *Julie After the War* . . . "

"*Julie After the War?*" he laughed. "Must have been some war."

She did not laugh, she stared. He cleared his throat and stood up. "Did I give you the black eye?" He looked around and frowned. He kicked the mop aside and walked down the hall, looking in the bedroom, the bathroom, and through the back hall he made his way to the kitchen. She was in the refrigerator pouring white wine in a glass.

[22] *Payofski's Dyscovery*

"Who hit you, Julie? Who gave you the black eye?"

She closed her eyes and drank the wine off. "You were sick."

He looked away and walked over to the table. The garden was pitch-black under the bright skyline. It was so quiet here.

"How many times?" he asked her image in the window. She did not answer. "I'm very sorry. Julie I am sorry. Maybe now that I have a new doctor . . . "

She turned with her eyes glistening. "I got paid tonight."

"Good," he nodded. "You frame pictures at the shop? Where is it? How long have you worked there? Are there benefits? When can I . . . ?"

"If you want, I could frame some of those . . . We'll sell some. Maybe. We'll find out what they're worth. Warren . . . "

"What's done is done," he said. "The paintings will have to earn their keep and we'll go out to dinner. I love you, Julie, I can just tell. What's our favorite restaurant? Do we sell my work often? You know when I walked in that studio, I *remembered*. I almost . . . remembered everything. You'll have to remind me what I charge . . .

"Julie?"

Inevitably he compared this life as a struggling artist with his brief life as a wayward man and inevitably he wished there were more differences. He did not think that the truth he had hocked his wedding ring for would be a life of near poverty, of loneliness or marriage to a girl who bewildered him. He never thought that instead of a life of certain failure, his failure was always imminent. He knew he was not a panhandler, but being grateful for that he did not realize his life was a life of debt, or that instead of the comforts of marriage he was more alone with a wife than he had been without one.

The very act of getting into bed with her had the strange effect of displacing her to the living room with a blanket, leaving him puzzled and ashamed. On the odd nights she stayed, he clung wide-eyed to his own edge and she clung wide-eyed to hers. But she had bathed and perfumed her breasts. Her nightgown was sheer. Delirious once, he reached to touch her hip but she jolted, whirling to glare in the darkness.

He would awake in their humid bedroom to find her gone. Sometimes she left him notes and food but mostly he had to content himself with traces of her—her lingerie in the cane rocker or her scent in the hall. She netted $119.54 a week at the shop and the white wine went down in the refrigerator like a barometer of everything she would not say. It was as

Payofski's Dyscovery [23]

if she stayed silent to see if he would be a better man after than he had been before, as if if she divulged his past he would feel responsible to it. The note she scribbled to him one day was like an omen. It said she had gone out to meet a man called Hector, the night shift supervisor at The Fort Point Frame Shop, and Christ, he thought. Hector who?

One day he said to her, "That tondo of Central Square dated last March. Don't you think that has genius?" And she leaped at him as she had at the police station. She wept with happiness; he buried his face in her hair. He staggered back with her legs as tight as a vise around his waist and when he tried to kiss her, she pushed him away. He stood, separated from her, furious. In the studio ten minutes later when he said he would attempt a landscape of the mountain—the mountain in the snapshot—she folded her arms and left the room. He found her in the wine again, with a jelly glass over the sink.

"No," she said. "I never saw that picture before. Please leave me alone."

Well, all right. He did. He went to the studio to stretch a canvas. It would be a huge painting, six by four feet, an American vista. He aligned his easel to catch the north light and mixed his paints. The excitement— he did not know if he could. Maybe his skills had fallen under the pall of the disease, or forgetfulness had gnawed away his vision. When he was ready to lay in the wash for the sky, his sponge poised and his breathing the slow fluxes of a marksman, Julie appeared in the doorway in a loose cotton dress with a low neck and a tortoise-shell necklace on her steep bosom. Folding her arms and looking between the window and him, she said, "There's a clean shirt on the bed, Warren. We're due at the hospital."

The hospital. So they went to the hospital together, both feeling alone. He wondered at the hospital and in galleries he would visit, when he was alone with her and not, if it had always been like this. A shapeless nurse breezed along the top floor of Mass General and covered his shirt with linen. "Beautiful day, isn't it?" she cooed as she buried a needle in his arm. His blood spattered the linen.

"Lovely," he looked away.

In this vein, through that needle, a red fluid dripped toward its mark, the lesion. He lay under the ceiling with his free arm behind his head and his crossed feet elevated. The fluid burned like acid. Julie sat against the wall flipping the pages of a magazine and looking up from time to time. Occasionally she scratched her arm. Because he respected Paley and the risks that men like Paley—artists—lived, Maurice Topsenfeld always swung by. He had told everyone the story of the ring. It was all over the hospital and curious nurses looked in on Warren Paley with his gyracinguloplasticchoreosis, studying the photo of the mountain he had taped to the IV bottle. The mountain he associated with something good in his life—something comfortable and carefree. It was only a mountain. But Dr. Topsenfeld lauded the association as therapeutically valuable. Greeting Julie and taking her cool hand, he did not tell his patient later his impression of a distraught woman with too much on her mind. Julie merely sat there, cool to Maurice, as if she would love Warren Paley even if it killed her.

So while I thought he was in California he was Maurice Topsenfeld's patient in Boston. Heat rippled from the macadam and hung in the landings and lobbies of the hospital. The bums he passed on the street, reminding him of what he had been, reached out to him and called him Payofski. "It's Paley," he would bark, balefully giving them change and cigarettes. Day and night he painted with a vengeance. Standing up like a conductor he painted with one foot on the rung of a stool. His arm reached in sweeping arcs across the sky of his huge canvas. Strokes of his brush laid a storm in the clouds. They were no longer summer clouds. No, it would be a winter mountain. He perspired and painted frost, the patch of his skull shaved for the electrodes gleaming with sweat. The blue of a winter sky appeared over the mountain. Sometimes Julie padded into the studio to watch. She was sipping iced tea on the sofa the morning he compared an abstract painted before his relapse with the mountain, and he threw his brush at the wall, put his fist to his head and said, "This is wrong. Damnation, this is wrong!"

She burst into shrill laughter. Her head went back and her breasts bobbed. Her mouth was open in helpless laughter, and his face burned like the sun.

"Get out of here!" he swore. "Get out! Out!" She turned white and fled, hiding in the bathroom, afraid, cursing herself, hallucinating the circle of faces and the blood on his suit. He had almost belted her. He stared at the wall in confusion and wondered that he had ever loved her, but the sight of *Julie After the War* shamed him and put him in his place. Sometimes he thought wistfully of the shelter, but no. They were married. There were vows. He would love her too, even if it killed him . . . .

I don't know when Julie first fell in love with him again—I mean for what he really was, the man he had been all her life. He was two weeks into the painting. His memory went back three and a half weeks and half of that he couldn't wait to forget. The crest of the mountain showed through blank canvas like the real thing through a cloud. The shaved patch of his skull he had taken to hiding with a Chinese straw hat he found in the hall closet. He worked feverishly. Julie had apologized and kissed him. She would creep into the studio to watch him paint and though he pretended not to notice her, his heart pounded. On her underwear little bears hung from balloons. The bears were brown, the balloons pink, and the panties yellow. It was late afternoon and he painted icy slopes of loess on his mountain as the bears grinned and hid the paradise he now longed for. He said, without stopping, "I want to talk to you about money, Julie."

She was silent a moment, then she said, "Good," and burped. "We don't have any."

"Then how do we manage? You bring home $119.54 a week from the frame shop," he said, "our rent is $475 a month, and you say I can't sell anything?" His lined face and blue eyes were serious. Julie looked out the window and down the street.

"Sometimes . . . Daddy sends a check."

He turned around on the stool, hands on his knees.

"Daddy?" he said. Paternal jurisdiction in the life of a middle-aged man?

"Oh, no more," she tugged her hair before her eyes. "You ended that."

"Good. Charity we don't need."

"He had us for a visit last year. You got mad at him for criticizing your work, for telling you you were a bomb as a painter. So you took me upstairs in his house and slugged me."

He dropped his brush in the glass. She was kneeling on the bolster and looking far down the street. The wail of a siren wormed its way across the channel into the room.

" . . . And he disinherited me," she added.

"I hit you—and your father disinherited you?"

"Two point nine million dollars," she nodded. "You were always at each other's throats and I was tired of being caught in the middle, if you want the truth. Two point nine million was getting off easy. It could have

[26] *Payofski's Dyscovery*

been a lot worse," she looked back over her shoulder. "It could have been three point one million."

"Yes," his voice was distant. "Three point one. Million." He stared at her backside. "What right did your father have to criticize my work in the first place?"

"He's a critic," she shrugged.

"I see. He's a *critic*."

"And a collector, who knows what he likes," she said. "And he doesn't like you."

"And a collector. How forgetful of me."

"You're being sarcastic."

"Forgive me. Does he by any chance paint?"

"He knows how. He isn't suited to the life of an artist. He doesn't have the ability," she stared hard, "or the stamina."

"I imagine painting bores him."

"No. He helps artists."

"How?"

"He gives prizes. He shows new artists. He owns galleries and publishes a magazine."

"New . . . "

"I told you," she said, lifting her tea glass, the color in her cheeks high and eyes over the rim, "I told you to stop looking to him, because he resents you."

"He resents me?"

"You're repeating me."

"Your father . . . " He looked away. He looked back. "Your maiden name is . . . ?" he put out his hand.

"Weir." She blushed.

"Weir," he said. "Weir." He slapped his thigh and stood and walked counterclockwise around the canvas. "Weir," he walked half around again, hitched up his pants and mounted three steps of the stepladder in the closet, reaching high to the shelf. There was the stack of magazines he brought down with a shoebox under his chin. His straw hat cocked awry, he dropped the magazines and the box on the floor at Julie's feet. It made a sound like a bomb.

"Your father is Allston Weir?"

Julie turned and gathered up her knee.

"Founder of *Artifact*?" he said. "Collector? The patron? The million-aire? The scholar? 'A.W.,' the author of this box of letters, is my father-in-law?"

"He kicked us out."

"You . . . "

"What?"

"You tack frames—on the night shift," he said, "for $119.54 a week. We live in a winery with a tin roof. Even now we're standing in a room full of the most innovative, the boldest . . . , " he spread his arms.

"Shit," she said.

"What . . . who . . . I paint shit? Who is he to . . . "

"Allston Weir," she scudded to the end of the sofa and stood. "You punched me. I told him to go to hell. I told him for you you were far too sure of what you were doing to beg anyone for help doing it. I told him he was jealous."

"Of my abilities. Good."

"No. Your abilities are shit, he said. He was jealous of you for want-. . . for marrying me."

"For mar . . . "

She padded out of the room with her I'll-be-right-back urgency, but she did not come back. She did not come back because his finding the box of letters terrified her. She was supposed to have burned the letters— Hector told her. She had forgotten. The closet was full of Weir's magazine, *Artifact*, the bible of the art industry at four dollars a month. Astounded, he ripped the Chinese hat from his head and slung it at the wall. The letters, found his first night home, had seemed unimportant. But now he sat back on the sofa, his temples pounding, his eyes wreathed in rage; he opened the box and pulled out the top letter.

Dear Julie,

Thank you for your letter and Warren's slides, which I am returning to you with my regrets. I won't mince words, Julie. Warren's work is hardly exceptional for a man of his years and training. He has a strong sense of color and space and some of his ideas are quite startling. He is innovative as you say—maybe too innovative. These abstractions are too abstract finally to be accessible, however.

On the plus side I can appreciate what he has done with *Duffy at the Ritz* and even cobalt blue for the dead color in *Eclipse of Sonja*—brash to say the least. In his calmer moods he can be quite sophisticated, but not very often. His ideas are strong—perhaps stronger than his vocabulary.

Thus I imagine his use of toothpaste to evoke breaking waves in *Notiluca Night Storm*, which fails in my opinion. Toothpaste? Julie, he should stick to paint.

I enclose something for your birthday, sweetheart. Buy a car with it or some furniture. I hope Warren is feeling better now. Please remember I'd do anything to help.

Once again I'm sorry about the slides.

Love, Your Father

He blanched in humiliation, folded the letter, flipping it back to the box. His shoulders slumped toward the floor and he clasped his hands under his chin. When he released his breath he went to the kitchen and brought a bottle of rye down from the cupboard and a glass and carried them back. The slam of the door echoed through the house and down the stairs. Julie, huddled in the bedroom, looked out at the dark street and cried again.

She was vulnerable to the feelings of both her sick husband and her charming and powerful father. She loved them both. The one had made her feel like a harlot, the other viewed her as a worldly possession. For too long it had fallen to her to mediate their mutual pigheadedness. In support of Warren's freedom to paint she had always cashed her father's checks, and it was not beyond her to spend some of the money on toothpaste. But for a long time now she had wanted nothing but escape and to find her sanity nights in wine, and days, each time Warren had dug out the letters from her father and obsessed, out in the market. She wore those aestival little briefs under loose skirts and blouses buttoned down to her breasts. She would sit under the trees with an ice cream, wishing she were someone else as she did when she was a child or serving silent judgment on the less-complicated looking women, I think because she wanted to be less complicated herself. Soon she would begin to hate the women and feel torn by the eyes of their men.

She had not made love to Warren for almost a year and I think that must have bothered him as much as the fact crushed her with guilt. This new Warren, purged by amnesia, an untried lover, was left to work out his lust on his painting of the mountain. Going from coffee to the painting without sleep, his shoulders drooped before the vista, his hair uncombed and hands stained, naive, trusting, he looked like a man more accustomed to climbing those mountain slopes than painting them. He rolled up his sleeves and lost himself, lost everything, this man with the bum memory.

In the act of being humiliated and deceived, living the painful life of Warren Paley, he had, or needed, the courage to be who he was at any given moment, and he worked and reviled Allston Weir.

One day he came home from the hospital and found Julie shut in the bathroom. The hair growing back on his scalp was fuzzy and gray. The bandage around his arm had crumpled and he felt tired and sick. He took a chair from the hallway and planted it in front of the door backwards. Straddling it, his arms folded on the back, he said, "It embarrasses me, Julie, not to be able to answer simple questions about my life and about you. I need your help in this. You've been hiding something from me. Something is wrong here. I want us to be friends. Let's talk."

Water splashed in the tub behind the door. Her voice was small. "All right."

He nodded. "Tell me how we met, please."

And she did, because she was afraid if she didn't he would not let her out. She reminded him that Concordia Academy for the Arts was founded by her great-grandfather. A collection of stone buildings and woodland, it stood in the Vermont hills. Painters and sculptors were enrolled there, actors and actresses who could weep on cue, composers who spent twenty hours straight in practice rooms only a little bigger than the baby grands. To a certain extent Julie Weir knew she would have been a trophy to any of these mad and creative people, on whom it was not lost that she was connected by blood to the institution that financed their dreams. I happen to know it made her very lonely. It probably helped her learn some of the wretched excesses of her time—how to drink alcohol and take speed and become secret and presumably resent her father, her name and her lack of choices.

Her years at Concordia were bad times for artists. Men like Allston Weir were considered saints by graduate students who thought that with a dinner date and maybe a smooch here or there, bingo. They would be the son-in-law of the most powerful man in the American art world. Allston Weir had clout and he had money and for better or worse he had a gorgeous daughter who dated whom she wanted, deriving, I think, the sort of pleasure a spoiled child gets from holding a magnifying glass between the sun and some insect. She had classified them. The sculptors went for her breasts every time. Painters went for her jeans. The pianists admired her teeth and held her hand. Poets gravitated to the woods. One day in the quad, tingling from diet pills and beer, she was painting a landscape when a man with a beard and eyes like flaring matches, a dirty coat and a violent face stopped behind her and stared at her canvas, an oil of the mountains in the distance. She was aware of him and turned. It was Warren Paley, and Warren Paley said, "That's wrong." He took a tube of acrylic orange from his pocket and squirted it all over the sky till it ran down the buildings and the grass. He slid the sleeve of his coat into his palm and messed the orange around exactly nine strokes, left, right, and down, and then stopped. "There," he said. And it was perfect.

Julie turned, wound up, and slapped him hard across the face.

Paley looked at her. He daubed his finger in the brilliant sunset and put a dab of orange at the end of her nose. "Go fuck yourself," he said, and walked away.

"Did I apologize?"

"No. Everybody knew Allston Weir's little girl was taking it up the bum from the only man ever to get kicked out of Concordia."

"Kicked . . . "

He heard her climb out of the tub and take the towel from the door. "You didn't care who I was. You'd give it to me good and tell me to get out and leave you alone. Or you'd have me over and tell me to take off my clothes and keep my mouth shut. I had a dream that he . . . that you . . . I—what I wanted from you. . . . Oh God go away," she said, "so I can come out and, because I've been everything you said, and everything *he* said and . . . ," she started to cry.

Three stories below the children wriggled in the gush of the hydrant and screamed in the heat. I remember reading in the paper that day it was a cool 65 degrees in northern California where he was supposed to be, but was not. He put the chair back against the wall, and walked down the hall to his mountain again, and shut the door.

"Dear Mr. Paley," he read on that fateful day, hunched forward on the sofa incensed, swigging from the bottle of rye, under great pressure. He pulled the Chinese straw hat down low.

Your sending me slides not two weeks after you visit my house, insult my staff and punch my daughter in the nose strikes me as phenomenal arrogance. If I recall our agreement was you would submit your most basic painting and that based on my opinion of it we might feature it in *Artifact*.

I happen to think these slides are no better than the others and they are probably worse. Nor, for that matter, did you improve the coloring or shape of Julie's nose. You make the mistake, Mr. Paley, of thinking that being my son-in-law entitles you to special dispensation in terms of your work. Then you have the nerve to criticize the way I brought my daughter up and the way I run my household. I think it's a pity she chose you for a husband, if this is the sort of thing you want to discuss, but that does not change my opinion of your talents with the brush and your vision. Both strike me as perverse and irrelevant.

I can no longer review your work without bias and have turned these slides over to my editorial staff. They will get back to you in the usual time.

"My staff," he gibed, "special dispensation," folding the letter into an airplane. He carried the plane between his fingers, struck a match and set it on fire, floating it out the window into the rain with a gloomy, forced smile. The letter glowed, soared, caught, burned, and fluttered to the street. He slammed the window and dusted his hands. At the end of the sofa in a bright red bikini bottom, Julie was reading a magazine. Her black T-shirt was torn off her shoulder. The raging man so sure of what he was glanced at her, then put his foot up on the stool to address his mountain, a problem he had encountered specifically—whether the silver or off gray would properly evoke a Pleistocene or a Holocene mountain. When he decided on the off gray and began to mix, Julie licked her finger and turned the magazine page. It made an annoying rustle, but when he turned to look at her the magazine was up before her face and her knee was raised.

He swirled his brush in the gray and the white again. Once again when his brush was poised she snapped a page across, moving her knee without looking. The rain began to fall hard, hammering on the skylight and roof. He lit a cigarette and stared out the window, and from the window to her, and the shadows at the crux of her thigh when she snapped another page across. He left the room for the kitchen where he poured himself a glass of water, swore, and took off his shirt and came back shirtless with his cigarette.

Silver would on the other hand evoke the slippery treachery of the north face, the danger of man's surroundings, the formidable power of God's rejection of man through His transcendence. Rejection, transcendence, sweat trickled under Paley's straw hat, dripping to his nose before he thumbed it away. Julie licked her finger, glanced at him quickly, and snapped the page across. The sound seemed to start at the base of his spine and shoot into his brain like a nail. He threw down the brush and left the studio for the bedroom where he took off his shorts. He came back in his briefs, then, with his cigarette and his hat. He stared at her from the door, but of course she would not look.

"No one can read that fast," he said.

She snapped a page across.

He left the studio for the kitchen, and this time he returned wearing only his hat. But he was not wearing his hat on his head. He stood in the door, looking at her, his back rippling with muscle and sweat, the sweat like jewels on his shoulders. His hands were on his hips. The straw hat was on its own.

"Julie," he said.

The magazine lowered. She looked from his face, to his body, to his hat.

"I want you," he said.

She slid down the other end of the sofa and stood up, backing toward the wall. "No," she said.

"I need you."

"No!" she padded out of the room. He followed her, methodically, purposeful, his hat swaying before him. "Julie," he said. She went into the living room. He went into the living room. "I need you."

"We can't."

"We're married. You're my wife. It's been more than a month since you saved me and I want to show my appreciation for this wonderful life we have together. You've been so forthcoming. Do you see this vase, Julie?" he lifted the crystal off the mantel. "Where did it come from?"

"It was a wedding present," she backed against the wall.

"It's full leaded," he weighed it. "And ten inches high. Look." He removed the hat and put his hat on his head. He inverted the vase over himself, giving Julie's eyes new cause for wonder for it was immense, swaying, and magnified now by the facets of the vase which hung free and upright like a buoy. His desire was a match for that weight and brilliant, a spectrum sprayed points of violet, purple and red light across the wall. The rain drummed the roof. "You see?" he said. "It hurts. I need to satisfy it in a civilized way. I love you more than anything in the world. This thing gets in a man's way. You must understand. When I feel like this . . . "

She slid down the wall and escaped. He followed her down the hall.

She backed into the kitchen and he navigated himself into the kitchen too.

"I'm your husband," he said. "I love you. You need me."

"Please don't."

"Do you see this jar of jam?" He picked the jar up from the pantry shelf. She backed against the range. "This jam satisfies you when you're hungry. It doesn't matter what it costs, if you like raspberries and you like jam, you'll buy it. Even if you don't like raspberries and you don't like jam, you'll eat this before you starve because you're human. You're alive. You'll find it quite delicious. Hunger, Julie. We're all we have, you and I, a man and a woman. Look." He took off the crystal vase. He unscrewed the jam jar lid and without taking his eyes off her, he overturned the jar and screwed it down to the bottom. The jam welled out with a long suck and dripped down to his thighs and from his thighs to his feet and he let it go.

It swayed.

"Oh God, no," she whispered and left the kitchen.

He followed, hands on his hips. The jam trailed him, the sweat glistened on his back and thighs and shoulders as he went down the hall and she turned behind the door of the bedroom and shut it. He stood politely at the door like a gentleman, bent double by desire.

"Knock, knock." He drew the jam jar back like a bow and let it fly against the door. "Open sesame, my bride."

"Please no."

He drew the jam jar back again and let it fly. The door had not latched and now it creaked open. "Ah," he said, entering, and he tiptoed in and stood over her. She was gathered up in the bed, staring up at him. "I love you," he said. "People miss being loved. Am I being selfish? Take off everything, please."

"I can't."

"You can. I'll help you. All right? See. Careful. Easy now. Knees together. That's it."

She looked at his eyes. He pressed her knees together and pulled the bikini from under her, then slid it over her knees. She took it down to her feet as he looked down and praised God's ingenuity. His knees trembled. She took the bikini off her toes and dropped it to the floor. She crossed her arms and pulled her shirt up, shaking her hair, her necklace and breasts free. He whispered, "It's coming." And she cupped the jar in her hands and lifted it. The jam dripped the length of him that pulsed and burned. It waved diamond hard and soft as velvet with a pulse. The moon stared through the clouds and skylight. A breeze blew in the curtains with the sound of the rain, and like a sprit bounding over a wave he hung over her. "Oh God," she whispered, and trembled as she girded his waist with her calves, and he knelt. She had dreamed . . .

"I love you, Julie."

He settled in, in. The jam welled as he descended. Cloven, her head thrown back, Julie sang an odd note and shivered. She threw her arms around him and searched out his throat with her lips. He closed his eyes in gratitude, it had been so very long. "I love you," he said; and she said, "I love you!"

Maybe Warren never did see Julie as a woman whose goal for eighteen years of her life had been to cause her parents grief. She had married a failed painter to wound her mother and spite her father, but when they awoke in each other's arms she whispered to him and he kissed her hair. They untangled themselves and shared their bathroom and breakfast.

If I may be allowed to ascribe to optimism a feeling of his own perfectibility, he felt perfectible that day. He collected his portfolio—a painting of a catatonic in a tent, a painting of a man on deck of a ship plowing a storm-tossed sea, a war painting and seascape—and set out with a little ruled book for the galleries. Up the best streets, those with the chicest shops and most glittery clients, he set out with the straw hat tilted over the bald patch, narrow green-banded sunglasses on, dapper in the pink jacket that had seen better days, tennis shoes and parachute pants tied around his ankles. His fat kelly-green tie blew in the wind and at the corner of his lips stood a dab of breakfast, Julie *avec de framboises*, delicious. He felt well. The wind blew against the big portfolio, clutched under his arm like a genoa jib. He was blown uptown.

His luck was hard, however. Failure had cast its black shadow over Warren Paley's days. The shop owners' and gallery guards' shabby treatment registered itself: "Paley? Out of here." "Fraud." "Show him the door." "Says he's who? What's he look like? Get rid of him." He was shown the back door, "Sorry," when he started to make a scene, "He's lying," demanding that at least the paintings be looked at, which they were not. And straightening his hat he wondered what was up here. Had Allston Weir's influence muddied Paley's future as well as his past? Did everyone read *Artifact*? Feeling perfectible yet, he felt blacklisted as well. The wind blew him down State Street and sent him careering backwards with the hat blown in his face, crashing into people whose burdens were perhaps lighter.

He went home in the afternoon discouraged. But soon his mountain would be done and men of affairs did not wallow. It was a powerful picture, redolent with winter firs. A stream ran at the foot of the mountain like a playful child escaping south. Lying on his back under the canvas, smoking, he said aloud, "You are certainly a democratic vista, a paternal image. Maybe I'll send your picture to Mr. Weir in secret, without telling Julie. I'll be humble and he will acquit me. If I grovel he might praise you in his fine magazine. We'll be rich." So perhaps too old to dream he dreamed anyway. The sunbeams came through the skylight and warmed him like a fetus in an incubator. He thought of his wife spreadeagle under him, sweet girl with luminous skin, gymnastic, growing exuberant, panting now, her little Mariposa tits aroused, squeezing him. He loved her more than he could bear.

When he awoke his cigarette had burned a rut in the floor and he cursed himself. A building like that, that kind of carelessness, you could kill two hundred artists in ten minutes. The competition would become fierce. He thought some suspicion arising from a dream that Julie was cheating on him had awakened him. He felt the flush of the cuckold rise in his cheeks and rubbed his eyes. And then another pebble cracked against the window.

He stood and went to the window and swore. Again—it was Simon Van Hyde and the giant, Christopher. He opened the window and shouted at them, "What do you want? Get out of here!"

"Payofski!" yelled Van Hyde. "We have news about your wife! She goes to the cemetery at . . ."

Payofski again! He whirled and stared around the room desperately, then ran out to the mantel and grabbed the vase. Running back, he stuck his head out the window.

"My name is Warren Paley!" he shouted. "Clear out of here or I'll call the police!" He fired the vase. Van Hyde jumped aside. Christopher didn't move or quit looking up. The vase exploded between his feet like an icicle and he shook his head to think of what he could have bought with it if he were quicker.

But the painter paced the room wondering again at his dream, how often Julie went out as she had that morning, her shirt open, conspicuous to the wind, her hair combed across her hot little eye. She said she was going to work, but did he believe that for a minute?

No—but he did not give up. In the ferocious heat of that ferocious summer he set out for the rude gauntlet of shop owners and gallery guards. When he had endured three hours of them in the afternoon he stood in the park where Van Hyde first talked to him and threw oyster crackers at the grass, his portfolio leaning against a silver beech tree. The light had the slant of autumn. He murmured to the pigeons who began to gather around. At last, an audience. "Fellow pigeons," he said, flinging them crackers. " 'Dear Mr. Paley,' " he quoted one of Weir's carrot-and-stick letters, acidly memorized.

> I cannot pretend to understand the uses to which you put your talent. What is this nonsense you send me? As much as you would have me believe you are ahead of your time, I run a business. My opinions are respected, and not, as you suggest, because I have lost any of the boldness which saw me to that position.
>
> If you still think you have something to offer us I insist it be something basic and clear—something that fits the realm of the critical language. Send me a horse, Paley . . .

A horse, Paley. He tossed a cracker to the pigeon he thought was in charge and hit him on the head. The pigeon flapped and ate the cracker. "If you had half a mind," he muttered, "you would see how basic I've been. A horse." He turned the cracker bag over and found himself ankle-deep in appreciative pigeons. They flapped and curred and fluttered as he waded away. "Idiot pigeons," he said, fishing his portfolio out of the flock. A horse. Julie said he had sent Weir the horse painting. He could not remember that he had. He did not have a slide of the horse. He had never found one workup of the damned horse. Setting out down the rose path for the hospital he saw, in the silvery grass under that autumnal light, a sunbathing woman. She was very thin. Her arm was raised and as a portrait she stunned him. He dropped his portfolio and framed her in his hands where he stood, his Chinese hat tilted and his eyes tight in thought. Her hips were like an invitation, two lithe hollows of light, and yet she seemed unassailable. That tiny suit civilized her. It was mysterious, her form with the little *pliers* and of course, hidden in the suit, the *Falltur*, supple and dark, boon, treasure and damnation of men. He moaned and picked up his portfolio and walked away, leaving her there as to God. This was the extent of his ego that day: Let God paint her. God had no desire. God did not want a God-damned thing. Was a man without desire perfect like God? Yes. A man without desire was perfectly dead.

"You're in a mood today," Dr. Topsenfeld said, laying the linen across the shoulder of a man who finally understood why hospitals kept people like him deep in the building, behind doors. "Where's Mrs. Paley?"

"Fine," he said. "Watch where you aim that thing."

Topsenfeld pushed the needle in. Blood spotted the towel.

"Don't talk if you're uncomfortable," said this man who prided himself somewhat, this impoverished doctor with the dandruff and shabby clothes, on pulling Paley out of the mire of anonymity. Why did the painter love him now? Topsenfeld taped the needle down and adjusted the flow of the red fire into a blue vein. "Is there anything else we can do?" The medical community, he meant.

"No. You're doing a good job."

"Thank you."

He was also in a mood, the doctor, and he went to the window and looked at his fingernails. "You're in a tough position, Mr. Paley. The odds against a happy life under these circumstances are high, but you're doing a good job. At any time you could relapse and everything you knew about yourself . . ."

"Would be wiped out."

"It's why I suggested a diary," Maurice turned back. "It reduces the risk of finding yourself alone, an inchoate man."

"Inchoate, yes."

"Your past is in the hands of others in a large sense—the hands of people who care for you. Who love you. It's up to them to help you preserve your continuity."

"That's true. What's inchoate mean?"

"You should have a bracelet with your name, at least."

"You told me. I've been busy."

Dr. Topsenfeld smiled. Then all expression fell from his face and he sat down in the chair by the bed. Suddenly he heaved a breath, drew back his coat and pulled out his gun, handling it like an expert, mesmerized by the nickel in the sunlight. "See this, Mr. Paley? This is a Smith and Wesson Model 18 .357 magnum revolver. Beautiful, isn't it?" The doctor turned it, holding it like a prosthetic limb of fear.

"Nice."

"Some people . . . Thank you. Some people think it's strange for a doctor to carry a handgun. But I collect guns," he turned it. "It seems to me a man can be this or that, now or then, anything, if he's smart, at any time given a certain set of circumstances. A man will adapt to what's thrown at him. For myself I love to heal people, and you know . . . I think I could kill anybody who tried to stop me . . ."

He held the gun and turned it for a long time, then sighed as if it did not matter and put it back in the holster. He rubbed his hands together and stood up.

"I have to go," he said. "Before I do, I want you to know something."

"Shoot."

"The latest scans show the lesion in your brain is healing. What this means," he clapped his prostrate patient's shoulder and smiled, "is that you're licking this thing."

Healing as Warren Paley, my poor friend leaned up on his elbows. He felt, looking at this doctor, as if the room had darkened except for him, Dr. Topsenfeld, who appeared to have the demeanor and attitude of a saint.

"Licked? It's gone?"

"It's going. It's up to you. Your spirits mean a great deal, Warren. You've taken to this treatment admirably and it shows. I want you to come back again next week. All right? You won't feel well, but we'll give the lesion one more kick. What do you say?"

"Say?"

He said yes of course. He walked home cheerfully as if a gallery had been opened in his name or he had died and become immortal. Each face he passed in the autumn light guiding him home was marked for a kiss. What difference did it make if the exertion sickened him? He bent to the porcelain altar of the toilet and threw up. He splashed cold water on his face and laughed. He checked in on his painting—the peaks that pricked his soul, the gorge, the overhanging western face and vertiginous snowslides. The $200 he and Julie had to their name was disappearing like sand through an hourglass, but he laughed and stripped off his clothes and ran a tub and sat back. His phallus floated like a buoy in the cool water; he flipped it from side to side with his hand, splashing, chuckling, dive-bombing the bubbles. He reached to the door and grabbed an issue of *Artifact* and floated it down to his feet, laughing till the pictures were sodden and he wondered that he had ever recognized a magazine that refused to recognize him . . .

He awoke much later with the skin of a prune. *Artifact* had dissolved and the bluish orange bathwater purled from his arms and shoulders as he sat up. There, on the mirror turned toward the tub, Julie had printed in soap.

No period now don't leave!

What? He pushed himself out and grabbed a towel and set out to find her—in the kitchen, the studio, the living room, the bathroom again. He found her in the bedroom asleep in the shop smock, her long hair fanned across the pillows, her palm up near her cheek. "My evasive little wife," he whispered, taking the glass from her hand, knowing full well that the night of the raspberry jam he could have fathered a universe. "You have to share more." She looked so peaceful he did not wake her though he put his hand on her belly, bending as though to feel the cells splitting toward a name, if it was true—uncoiling nothingness becoming his son or his daughter. He hoped. In his studio he raised his fists to the ceiling and turned up his face and whispered, "Cured? And a baby. Everything will get better! Everything will!"

And after all this—her deceit and evasions, the lies and left-handed machinations of Hector's plan—it came to a head. One week later he went to the hospital with a prayer that the insurance policies of the Fort Point Frame Shop could bear up under the strain of his gyracinguloplasticchoreosis and a baby too. He walked downtown with a box of slides, and up all those flights to Maurice, who stared down through the window at the roaring, thundering, dilating city. "So," he said, "you'll keep a diary?"

The blood spurted.

"Yes."

"I was wondering . . ."

"What? Ask anything, Maurice. You'll have a statue on the Esplanade before I'm through with you. I'll see to it. I have a painting I want to give you."

"I won't take it."

"Nonsense. Give me a gun for it, if you have to. A little one. We wouldn't want to start anything."

"We'll see. I was going to ask if you felt your wife has been thoroughly honest with you. You've picked a hard life. Art . . . medicine has clear goals. Obstacles to overcome one at a time," he turned the cock of the IV. "Painting—music and literature, I imagine—in those things one doesn't have to be present to win. You'll need your stamina. Not that I know that much about it."

"You know, Maurice. Don't be modest."

"I would think this sort of life leaves one feeling cut adrift. I'm curious whether you feel very alone."

"Julie is with me all the way," he said. The tube burnt like hell. Maurice shambled over and stared at a spot on the floor before he looked up. "What I'm getting at is your state of mind, Warren. If you can't keep your spirits up, then this treatment . . ." He raised his hand, dropping it in a gesture of futility.

"I'm fine. Believe me."

"What you need is to reminisce. Remember. Every day is a victory if you remember just a fraction of it. This country . . ."

"You're in a mood."

"We've become a nation of followers and damn the rest. Little headphones and tinted windshields. Alarms and tire irons. Steel grates and members only. We exclude ourselves. I wish . . ." he looked down at his patient. "I wish I could tell you that your genius doesn't reside in your hippocampus, an organ subject to disease like any other. If this therapy could restore your genius, Warren, I think I would get on that bed with you and we would burn together." The doctor laughed. The lining of his coat pocket was torn and waved like a flag of surrender.

"But genius is disease, Maurice. The goal is immunity! Buck up. I'll live! I think Julie's pregnant. You're a great man. Take it! Be happy, Maurice."

So for the last time he burned and believed Julie was being honest with him and that good things could come from a life led with a sense of destiny. He left the hospital virtually cured but warned. He climbed the hill to Joy Street, down Joy to Beacon to Arlington and the Newbury cafes. The sky was vivid blue. Puffy clouds cruised east in a regatta as he walked. The sun gilded one side of that posh street and left the other in shadow.

Passing a cafe with white tables and umbrellas and potted plants, he turned around and commandeered a table at the edge. Next to him was a table of four women sipping drinks. They were nice to look at, they and their libations. The waiter was a boy with wavy hair and tight trousers who took his order for a Devil's Tear and brought it along. The ladies were dressed in sleeveless shirts and cocoa tans, designer sunglasses, deep bronze shoulder blades as smooth as ice cream, and skirts that fretted in the breeze. A pile of tens was anchored by the ashtray. Sometimes one or the other glanced at him, framing her chin in her fingers. These four had drunk from the wells of beauty and laughter; they knew the power of their nakedness, no doubt. They were lovely, fashionably bony, self-assured. Why did Julie not have friends like these? he wondered, and downed the Devil's Tear and ordered another as he took out his slides.

The booze improved them. He had taken a picture of his mountain and not even the vodka and triple sec could free him of some fear that his work was not what it once was. "One day," he said, "Mr. Weir will see what I've done, the fool. Who does he think he is?" The lady in red tipped her sunglasses to the tip of her precipitous nose. He waved at her as if she were a thousand miles away. As she passed her little smile on to the others they passed it around. Were they making fun of him? His penis turned over in his lap like a baby porpoise and soon crippled him.

Well he was not going anywhere now, and he ordered another drink. Topsenfeld had given him some cannabis for the nausea. He drew out a slender cigarette from his pocket and sniffed it, running his nose down the length, lighting it and leaning back. He turned his face up to the sun. He puffed and held the smoke down deep, his cheeks blown out like a pufferfish, his slides spread out on the table. That all the cars along the curb were foreign and upside-down seemed a profound observation. "Sir? *Sir!*" It was the waiter knuckling the steel white table. "Please put that out."

The artist put his head back and looked up. The waiter was upside down also. "Put it out why?"

"Because it's against the law is why."

"But it's medicine."

"It's marijuana."

"It's medicine. I have a prescription." He stuck his fingers in his pocket and pinched the piece of paper, the phone number of the Washington Street Shelter for Wayward Men. He tossed it deftly in the air.

"You have no right to interfere with my therapy. Go away. Go ask those lovely ladies what they want."

"It's against the law."

"It's medicine. This bandage around my arm did not come from Saks. I don't cut my hair this way, the goddam nurses do. Don't you know me?"

"No."

"Neither did I. Thus the medicine. Now fix me another Devil's Tear, hipso fatso. And a round for the brown ladies."

"That's it," the boy said. "You'll have to leave."

"Oh?" He lay his head back. "And why is that?"

"Up. I have to."

"You'll have to have to first. Well—all right. If you have to be an ass." He stood up and shuffled the slides together. The ladies passed around their smile. "My name is Warren Paley," he said, sipping the last of his drink, straightening the bandage on his arm. "I am an artist! When my authorized biographer gets in touch with you, you'll be sorry. He'll blacken your name forever. You won't get a sketch of mine on your miserable tablecloth for less than the price of that limousine." He put his slides in his pocket, tamped the pot on the tabletop and tweezed it into his pocket. "Obviously doesn't know who I am," he told the women. "Philistine—asking me," he tapped his chest, "to put out my cigarette. I'm Warren Paley, for God's sake! I have a growth!"

But he reeled out from between the table and chair and threw down some bills. "A gratuity for you, my little tyrant. No hard feelings." He kissed the waiter on the mouth. The bills blew away.

On he went. Down the glittering street the sunlight was keen on a man who'd drowned more than his nausea in smoke. The gallery windows were remarkable if rather egregious failures, to his eyes. "Unconvincing perspective," he said, pausing to frame the pictures in his hands. "Manneristic. Contrived. Old-fashioned. Improperly laid-in. Amateuristic. Did better when I was three." He stormed past window after window. "Ah, *nature morte*. An udder in a hazel sky. And only $5,000. Asinine!" He spoke to his reflection and pressed his face to the window. "From the estate of Mrs. Carlotta Squiggles, under execution of Eugene Fairweather. He owns the self-portrait of Orazio Gentileschi, if memory serves. *Caravaggio's Protégé*. Good for him. Hello, my friend." He stormed on. Past boutiques he went, a failed painter with a knocked-up wife. He caught his reflection in a window display of alpine gear, his hair shorn to the sensors, the straw hat jammed down, his jaw thrust forward like a man threatened by himself. Beads of sweat popped out on his forehead, a man in charge of a secretive wife and the human tadpole therein. Me, he thought, a father? He grinned. Finally it hit him. He pulled out the cannabis and lit it and marched down the street with the sun in his eyes. Shadows of people moved past. Sometimes a man felt sainted by his failures, wearing them in his mind like a thorny crown. No man was good enough to please everyone—or was it bad enough? Who cared? There was freedom either way.

I am a father, he thought, I must be. I feel it. God has not abandoned me. What irony to have married the daughter of a man whom all these people had elected umpire of their symbols of beauty. People stared at him and he nodded hello, hello, nice to see you, hello. They stared as if he were mad. His smile was mysterious and sporty. His trousers, baggy and untied, luffed in the wind. The smoke filled his cheeks and when he let it go he stepped in front of an elegant black woman who tried to sidestep him, and kissed her on the mouth. "I love you," he said, "no hard feelings," holding her shocked. "I've always loved you, remember?" He kissed her sumptuous mouth and walked away. She said nothing. A father!

He crossed a busy intersection now, anxious to be home again with his wife and speak to her. Descending stairs under the street he slid a bill to the man in the wicket and leaped the turnstile for the trains. His breath heaved. It was cool under ground but he perspired wildly and his blood hammered in his ears. There was a man leaning against a pillar in the dim light of the billboards and tunnel. "Payofski?" said this man, stretching out his hand. No—remember your wife and your health, your success. There was no more fertile and hallowed a ground to plant his seed in than her. He was *not* a failure. Failures did not have children. The train exploded in the tunnel, a Cyclops of strobing lights that froze people, faces and newspapers. The doors sucked open. He boarded, doomed, seizing the grip as the doors sucked closed and the train jerked.

Moreover, he thought, swaying, smiling, I am free. A man has to live, a man has to follow his instincts. He shut his eyes as the train roared. He seemed to be amidst an audience of people buried in newspapers and Topsenfeld's little headphones. He pictured Julie rounded in eight months by the baby, her breasts lachrymose, her walk a waddle. Past six stops he went and then the doors sucked open on more people to love. Up the stairs he ran squinting in the light, rounding a corner for the bridge, smiling, hello, hello. I mean you no harm. We're doing fine. I remember everything, Saint Maurice, thank you! The bridge was a steel grate and below the channel water sparkled. Fatherhood. I'm going to be a father. What do you think of that, Weir—fatherhood! Take that! What defiance! What a blow to the enemy!

He turned down his littered street and mopped his head. He went up the stairs of his decrepit building to his landing, his home. He stopped. He was about to call out to Julie when he heard voices behind the door. He held his key close. One was Julie's. The other was some man's.

"You were supposed to have him ready! Where is he!"

"He's not here!" Julie screamed. "Get out! Out!"

"It starts in half an hour! Where is he!"

"I *hated* your brother!" Julie screamed. "I *hated* him, Hector! Get out! Get out!"

He opened the door. The man inside backhanded Julie, knocking her to the floor, and he spun to aim a little nickel and ivory gun at his mark and said, "Freeze, Weir! Get in here! Move one step and I'll kill you!" Indeed. Ally shut the door behind him calmly and faced this man.

Julie screamed in tears, "Hector!" her face streaked. "I told you to leave him alone!"

"Shut up, you! If you're not up to it I'll do it myself! What the hell do you think I've been waiting for?" That spat out, he stepped back, waving the gun in both hands between Julie and the gentleman in the hat. That man, holding the hat before him now, placating Hector with a look of benign confusion, tried to draw some conclusions quickly. The gunman was pale, nervous, skinny, five-ten with freckles and pinched bald eyes. This was no conclusion. He had a sunken chest and ponytail fetched up in a copper Turkshead. "You!" he hissed. "Inside! Back out to the stairs! Don't move!"

"Anything you say . . . Hector, is it?"

"Shut *up!*" He screwed up his face. "Mr. *Weir*, you ass! Think you're good enough to take my brother's name? You are *nothing!* You paint like a monkey!"

"Who are you? And if you have a better idea, who am I?"

"Shut up!"

"Hector," Julie yelled. "No!" Hector took a jump step forward and whipped Weir on the head with the gun. He—Payofski, Paley, Weir—doubled over and looked up stupefied.

"Don't move!"

"I know. You said that."

"Daddy!"

Hector whirled and aimed the gun at her. "If you try to stop me I swear I'll kill him."

"You," he said out the side of his mouth, "outside downstairs. There's a car at the curb. Get behind the wheel!" On the floor Julie was sobbing. Her skirt was thrown up over her thigh, which broke Allston's heart. But she seemed unhurt and he did as Hector said—opened the door and walked out. Hector shoved him against the banister, across the landing and down the stairs. Hector—he must have worshiped his brother. The hours he did not spend at the Fort Point Frame Shop he spent writing elegiac poetry about Warren. He spent most of his money from the shop on Valium and heavy rag paper on which he had his poems photocopied and mailed to himself via the national publishing houses. The process seemed to have disturbed him. At the bottom of the stairs he cracked the puzzled man on the head. Julie's voice echoed down the landing as he shoved Weir out to the street to a beat-up orange Kharmann Ghia, a wreck of rust and seagull shit with no muffler. Allston got in behind the wheel, and beside him Hector yelled, "Drive, murderer!" and tied his door shut with a hank of rope.

So Allston drove. Why, where—in his confusion there seemed no time for these questions. He drove with his head reeling from the vodka, the pot, the pistol and three identities as Hector peppered his directions with insults and exhortations to make the orange shitbox get along. Allston Weir? he thought. It had to be a lie. The car reeked of gasoline and glue. It belched oil and backfired. "Excuse me," said Julie's father, "but did you say murderer?"

"Shut up and drive!"

He jammed it in third gear. The little car boiled and belched under an overpass, tearing with a whoosh between two pushcarts, then through a light onto the boulevard paralleling the river west. Hector punched him in the head and cursed him. When they had gone three or four miles he told him to take the ramp south, then he beat him on the shoulder and the car careened against a concrete barrier. Sparks flew. Recovering the car, Payofski saw stars. He tried to collect himself and think. "I am being kidnapped. Julie knew something about it. Who am I?" What a question!

The exit issued on a square congested with eight lanes of traffic and with that Hector grew calm. Allston looked over and tried to gauge his chances, but escape was impossible. The next street was the street the gunman was looking for, a dead end lined in trees. He laughed. He roared insanely. "Pull up to the curb and park it!" he cracked Weir on the head.

"I have a question if you don't mind."

"Shut up and park, you sick bastard! Get the blood off your face! Look presentable!"

Weir parked and clenched the wheel and looked straight ahead. A drop of blood rolled down his forehead. Hector reached to the back seat and yanked a brown bag up.

"Put these on."

"Of course. Anything." Julie—he prayed for her, three or four words. In the bag were a rumpled black tie and wool houndstooth check jacket. Wrenching around into the jacket he saw that Hector was watching the building across the street, a posh Georgian mansion cloaked in ivy. There was a big foyer with a chandelier. The doors were open on a doorman and a bar. Inside, well-dressed men and women were drinking champagne. Now and then some of them broke off and went into the main hall, which seemed to descend like a horizon. The hall and foyer looked cool and dark—some sort of auditorium, Paley thought—a convocation, a baptism, maybe a funeral. Mine? The indignity of his gyracinguloplasticchoreosis came back to him with full force. Whatever was going on inside involved fabulous amounts of money. "Straighten the damn tie," Hector bellowed, and laughed again. He laughed with his eyes shut. "What the hell kind of haircut is that, anyway?" It seemed he laughed for ten minutes. Allston wanted to explain; he wanted a few minutes of peace and someone to tell him the truth. It was useless. When Hector aimed the gun at his head the foyer of the mansion was empty and the bar was closed. Whatever was scheduled had begun. One needed information, Weir thought. What have I done to this young man? He watched waves of heat shimmer on the car hood and the sails on the river. Before long Hector seemed to stop breathing and to count backward. He fell very still. "Now," he said, and reached to the back seat for a jacket, which he put on over the T-shirt advertising the night shift at Fort Point.

"When we go in, *Mr. Weir*," he gritted his teeth, "you get your paddle from the doorman. It's number eighty-seven. Can you remember that? Can you! You follow me down the center aisle. And you smile, you son of a bitch! Smile!"

It was, somehow, Payofski's smile. It looked all wrong. Hector grabbed the black tie and yanked Weir's face close. *"Get the blood off your face, you geriatric jackass! You do what I say in there or I'll shoot somebody. I don't care who! You could have helped Warren! You could have helped him and you didn't! Do you understand!"*

"I think so."

He slammed his way out of the car and marched around. The gun was in his jacket pocket. He smiled graciously as he opened the door for Weir and they crossed the street together. "Beautiful day, isn't it?" Hector grinned. The stranger looked dazed and yet he smiled, utterly confused.

Sick and lost, Allston went down the middle aisle that day with no sign of the beating he'd taken, ill-dressed in Hector's jacket and his sneakers but with reputation enough as a wealthy man that no one cared. So it had all come down to this, a protracted act of revenge, and no one was more surprised or speechless than he was. Above him the lights were dim. A couple of New York cognoscenti nodded to him crookedly, for they had met this famous recluse once, and he had always sported a full beard. They nodded at the long-haired gentleman who walked alongside him. Some people waved uncertainly and Allston waved as uncertainly back, searching for a face he might know. At the first two empty seats in the middle aisle Hector nudged him. Down front was a stage with a proscenium arch and a man in black tie at a lectern with a microphone. In a mellifluous voice this man was announcing Lot 22, a Pier Francesco Mola offered in lot with a coprolite, crafted, the catalog said, by Tutankhamen. Both *objets* were rolled onstage by a girl of nineteen or twenty, heavyset in a yellow dress with a soupcrock hairstyle. The hall lights were low, and soon after the introduction of the Mola and fossil the bidding began.

Hector stared forward from the aisle seat, stiff and perspiring. His anguish had reduced itself to a twisted smile. His lips were bloodless. His hands clenched the catalog on his knee and the man, stranger to himself, turned to find that of all things he felt sympathy for this neurotic. But then a man in the row behind tapped him on the shoulder and whispered, "Good to see you again, Mr. Weir. Your beard . . . forgive me. You're looking well." Weir stiffened and nodded without turning.

Before he understood what was happening the Mola and the turd leveled off at $13,600 and the auctioneer dropped his gavel. The paddles fanned the people who were not as interested in that lot as in Mr. Weir. They supposed this was some introduction of the ponytailed man, some protégé perhaps. A great artist? Another lot preceding 41 was a silver sixteenth-century bell and the bidding was long and Hector became agitated. He seemed about to erupt again—to pummel Allston on the head. But then the auctioneer said, "Lot 41.

"An oil painting," sipping from a water glass, "on unstretched canvas, by Warren Paley. Educated at Concordia Academy for the Arts, at age thirty-eight Mr. Paley was awarded the prestigious Bonne Chance Ribbon of Artistic Excellence, from which he took, in his own words, 'the license to break the Post-modernist mold and paint the territory of the subconscious according to the laws of reason.' For this Mr. Paley primarily broke from his peers, and this painting, *Bertrand's Horse*, is considered his foremost example. It is believed to be the artist's last work.

"The bidding will begin at $500."

When the pretty apprentice unveiled *Bertrand's Horse* it was to some laughter and Hector looked, now, confused himself. The murmurs began in the front row and rolled to the back. In the back a man disappointed with his view laughed louder than the rest in a tone that dismissed the whole thing. The murmurs made their way down front again and broke over the painting like a wave. *Bertrand's Horse* was indeed a painting of a horse. As for representations of horses it captured the grace, I suppose, the power, the scope, the wildness and the lust of an untamed animal. It was a horse executed with derangement, a stallion that looked ready to fly; it was sleek. The laughter, the ridicule, had its source in the landscape in which the horse was painted. The horse—it was standing on the moon.

Weir stared forward, bewildered. He saw the horse. He saw the moon-dust, the night and the star-blasted sky. The horse's shoes kicked up the dust. The mane and tail were lifted. What caused the stir was perhaps not the horse but the oxygen bottle strapped to its throat. Over its nose it wore a mask. More—worse—the horse's eyes were crossed. Crossed. Even the man in the back saw the horse's crossed eyes through his opera glass and the joke began to spread. Five hundred dollars? Some people bowed their heads in embarrassment; some made faces and fanned themselves.

Not Hector. He sat there, an island of gravity with his jaw clenched and his heart beating tattoos in his veins, and leaning to his left he jabbed Weir and hissed, *"Bid."*

"What?"

"Bid! Bid!" Hector jabbed his arm. Weir lifted the paddle. Hector nudged his arm higher and as the people looked down at paddle number eighty-seven, the auctioneer acknowledged the bid.

"I wouldn't trade your moosehead for that, Calvin," a woman was heard to say. But no sooner did she open her mouth than a woman down front raised her paddle and upped the bid for the cosmic horse. Viciously Hector smiled. The auctioneer turned the page and read, "Mr. Paley's mechanical rendering of life's great joke led him to impose on his style the belief that the subconscious could be mapped and that it was the metaphor that was essentially the thing. He sought to wrest art from the realm of the actual and material, and plant it squarely in the realm of the real, thus to make the actual the metaphor . . ."

A man behind Hector said, "The realm of the real?"

"Bid," Hector hissed, "or you're dead."

"The actual, the met- . . . as in you, David?" the man's wife said with disdain, her glasses lifted to look and be sure the eyes of the horse were crossed, since they did not look so crossed now as before.

"Insane," someone said. Heads bent to heads and whispered, "Mr. Weir is bidding."

"Preposterous! Imagine that next to Manet?"

"Bid!"

The woman down front raised her paddle.

"Mr. Paley's abstractions, painted before *Bertrand's Horse* was commissioned and refused by Allston Weir, met with little acceptance the last ten years of his life. Scorned by his contemporaries, he pressed on with his theories of subordinate reality—of a reality conditioned by the symbols which interpret it . . ."

"But the realm of the real?"

"Winston, the Bonne Chance Ribbon for Artistic Excellence gives a prize of twenty-five dollars, doesn't it?"

Under the gentle hand of the soupcrock girl, who wondered in the laughter if her slip were down, the horse's eyes crossed and uncrossed. Iconoclasm turned hallucination in the whispers. Nothing seemed so lasting as that Warren Paley had lived and died a madman. The stars gleamed with an intensity that exceeded white; the painting looked perforated, held up against the sun or some spinning engine. Another paddle went up—neither Weir's nor the girl's down front—and Hector jabbed Weir, "bid!" Another. "What do you think?" arose. "I don't." "Bid," floated in whispers, buoying the name and cherished judgment of Allston Weir, for twenty years lessor of paddle eighty-seven. A program was thrown onstage and there came the usher. Through the backstage door the rotors of a police helicopter paddled the still air above the river.

"Outrageous! Why that's not art! Is it?"

"No. But don't quote me."

People who found it ridiculous looked at those who wondered if it was important. Those who thought it important wondered who was more entitled to judge. A rep-dressed gentleman and his rhinestoned wife put their heads together and raised the paddle for a bid of $1,500. To the right a man said, "A brief review in *Artifact* not four months ago dismissed this Paley as a fraud, a casuist, and by all accounts a pederast with left-wing tendencies."

"Well," said his wife, "bid!"

So it was slowly but grudging the momentum of Allston's determination to buy that the paddles came up. Weir faced Hector placidly and no more believed he was Allston Weir than he could dispel the hope he was not. Tears were brimming in Hector's eyes. The bidding climbed over three thousand dollars and as it edged toward five thousand another wave of paddles joined, waving it toward six thousand and the weird infamy of works executed by artists who had died without a name. Down front Penny of the Fort Point Frame Shop, the second confederate in Hector's plot, put her paddle on her seat and slipped out by the fire escape. Hector looked hard at Weir with the bliss of hatred and jerked his head as a sign for him to follow him outside. Now.

Outside Weir squinted in the harsh sunlight. He did not understand. He was unsure of his position, his assets, of whom he was supposed to love, to fear, or to trust. The cut had clotted at his hairline. The houndstooth jacket drooped on his shoulders. Humiliated, speechless, he stood under more accusations of murder, of theft, by mad Hector. Then Hector stopped. And Hector smiled and turned white and pulled his pistol from his coat.

"This is from Warren," he said and put it to Weir's chest point-blank and shaking. "I loved him, damn you!" and as the gavel dropped to a bid of $10,000, Hector shot him.

Celeste and
the Art of Money

That's how Allston came home to us after nine weeks—nine weeks in which we believed him to be on the West Coast undergoing a cure for the lesion. When it became clear to me that he never got there because of a relapse, I suspected any number of people had tried to capitalize on the symptoms of innocence and gullibility associated with forgetting. But only God knew, perhaps, besides Julie, and you who remember, that he was there when Warren Paley flung himself off the skyscraper.

Finding out that he had not gone to California threw his wife, Celeste, me, and his house in Vermont into confusion. Celeste, a high-strung auburn-haired woman of forty-five, could look twenty when she was pleased with herself and sixty when everything was going wrong. I happened to be there when she got the call from Boston and she dropped into her Louis XIV chair in the piano room and commenced to look sixty-one.

I caught a plane to Boston immediately and arranged to have Allston driven home to Vermont in an ambulance. On my return I found Celeste staring at the fireplace.

"They missed," I told her. "The bullet entered the chest near the shoulder. He's all right."

She frowned. "They haven't caught the man yet?"

"No, but they have a description."

She crossed her arms and curled her fingers under her chin and stood. The scarlet silk pants suit she wore was expensive and detailed as were all her clothes. Her color was high as she stared down at her gold pen on the table, her glasses and emery board, the Egyptian forward curl of her hair at her cheek scending in the light. "Nine point nine million dollars," she said, and stared at me. She put out her hand. "Don't look at me that way, Foster. How will a man in his condition manage now? He's had another relapse, hasn't he. Is he dying?"

"I don't know. We'll test him."

"Oh shit," she slapped the pen and paper off the table and walked to the window in little steps. "Do you know how embarrassing this is?" she turned. "God knows where he's been. All this time he's in 'California,' taking the cure. Not a word, and you thinking it was just his stubbornness because you couldn't recommend it. What a load of . . ."

"Maybe you want to know something about his condition," I said. She was staring out the window—no answer. "He's coherent, Celeste. He seems to know who he is and where he's been. He even knows the name of the man who shot him, but he wouldn't tell the police."

She didn't turn at this. "How many times have you told me there's no cure for what he has?" she asked. "Were you wrong?"

"I never said absolutely there was . . ."

"You did," she said. "You did."

There—etched in stone. I looked out through the étagère at the window. She'd had some statute of limitations in mind, or a fantasy he wouldn't come back. She had had such plans for it, too, the money. For the sunlight that rolled across his estate. I could almost read her mind. She turned to me. The slightest motion set the silk suit shimmering. Around her neck concentric gold chains scattered the light as she walked back to the chair and sat, arms folded, her legs crossed, her sandal dangling. She felt sorry for herself and thought it unfair of me to sympathize with him now.

"He'll need to be in the hospital, I suppose."

"No."

"Oh, Foster," she brushed the velvet arm of the chair, silk rippling, gilded celerity and beauty like a big gem in the room. "Don't sit there in judgment on me. Don't judge me in that Tom Dooley Father Teresa simpering holier-than-thou baritone bullshit tone of yours, ten million dollars . . ."

"*Shhh.*"

"*Ten million dollars*—is not nothing to you, damn you and your hypocritical oath."

"It's 'cratic, Celeste."

She stood, moving toward me, standing over me. "Two months playing house, feeding from my open hand in front of the staff. Aren't you brazen," she turned away. "Hand?" she raised hers to the window and let it fall.

"We have to be reasonable now," I said. "Be yourself. Nothing's changed."

"Except that your career is back," she turned. "Your ticket to Stockholm on a damned theory of the seat of the memory of self. Your great challenge! I know I take a back seat to his glorious disease."

"Enough. Do you think I would have kept on with this arrangement for twenty-five years if you didn't matter?"

She turned on me again, all silk, gold and vitriol. "A man doesn't have to be a doctor to count to ten. Or especially romantic to tack six zeros on the end, Foster."

God, what a woman. Her beauty was artifice, her sex was rhetoric, her contacts tinted according to the Paris magazines and she had the art of money down pat. Celeste and the art of money. She was more single-minded than I; she knew better than to think my devotion to curing Allston could be bought, and that infuriated her. At the same time I knew it was what fascinated her about me. But whether she liked it or not Allston was home. And he did not need to be hospitalized. He had had a relapse. He had had them before. Occasionally she liked to make a run at it—my devotion. Even then she smiled down at me, sitting back in the chair and crossing her legs. "I believe it's time you looked in on him," she said, and she looked out the window as if I had already left.

I went up to the west wing. He was in the gold bedroom staring at the Franz Kline on the wall. The expression he turned to me wasn't exactly trusting. He seemed angry. (At the time it seemed irrational to me.) The codeine had left rings under his eyes. His hair was long, which I was not used to. "Hello, Allston," I said. "Do you recognize me?"

He stared hard for a moment, squinting, then shook his head.

"That's understandable." I took the chair at the foot of the four-poster. The terrace curtains were closed and the room was dark. "My name is Foster Ames," I told him, "your doctor. You and I go back a long way. There's probably a lot you want to know about your condition. And yourself. You seem to have had a rough time. A man shot you, as you know." He looked away in thought, a posture of having command over the situation. He thought I was lying. "You should know your health is good, not counting the bullet wound. You have a dysfunction of the brain, Allston . . ."

"I know."

"The problem . . . is in the cells between the hippocampus and the amygdala. It's rather complicated. What it does is leave you blank at times, which isn't easy, I know. Not easy getting along without the right information," I smiled. "The important thing is you're home. This is your home. I can promise you that gradually you'll begin to remember again. Now is there anything I can tell you right away?"

"My name."

"Allston Lloyd Weir," I stood up. "You're forty-four years old. Your wife's name is Celeste. She's downstairs until you're rested. You have a son, too. Named Bertrand."

"Only a son?" He put his head back.

"No, you have a daughter, named Julie. There was a falling out with Julie some months ago. You disowned her, as any self-respecting father would have."

He nodded and looked away, his jaw clenched. "And what is my occupation?"

"You're a patron of the visual arts and a collector. You own galleries in New England. You finance shows across the country and award grants to promising artists. You collect commissions on sales of paintings featured in a monthly you founded in 1972. You're an opinion-maker. A very respected man."

He turned back to the Franz Kline.

"What do you know about where I've been?"

I shrugged. "You left here nine weeks ago for California, and a treatment, which I urged you not to take, frankly. You were found yesterday afternoon outside the Hilliard House in Boston. Shot."

"What else?"

"Do I know? Nothing. Your family and I . . ."

"Warren Paley," he said suddenly. "Where is he?"

"Warren . . . is dead, Allston. He fell off a building two months ago.

I meant to tell you as soon as you got back." He nodded, his mouth tense. "We were all very worried about you, Allston."

That was especially true of Bertrand, his son, though Allston again looked at me as if it were a lie. It had fallen to me to explain to Allston's seven-year-old son that his father had forgotten everything again and been shot. Bertrand had his father's large eyes and high forehead. Like his mother he had a second face for the formality of manners. He thought I meant that someone had punished his father for forgetting and it seemed to both frighten and amuse him. He wanted to be the first to see his father, yet Allston turned to me and gave me that dubious smile as if to say maybe he didn't really have a son, or prove to me this is my house. He was suspicious, but the boy was his.

"I'd like to give you something to help you sleep, Ally."

"Call me Mr. Weir, if it's not too much trouble. And I'm tired of sleeping."

"We've been friends since graduate school." His rebuke stung. "I was best man at your wedding. Perhaps we can find some time to talk about what happened in Boston?"

"It's none of your business."

"I see."

"Any reason we can't open those drapes?" he pointed.

"No, let me."

I loved him (pardon the sentiment). Allston Weir had paid a high price for what he was, for what he had made of himself and knew. He was successful, handsome and rich; he succeeded at everything he ever tried in life and he excelled. He never failed at anything and that made him easy to resent. I may have loved Celeste because she was his. I was even a little afraid of him. He broke my arm once, a greenstick fracture. He didn't like to be disagreed with and he didn't like to be wrong.

I went to the terrace doors and opened the draperies. The sunlight spilled across the bed. When I turned to him he was squinting again. He was shaking his head. From that room the view of the estate was heady. Cardinals nested in the maple trees lining the drive and skirred over the grass. The lane wound from the carriage house to a black iron gate that fronted fifty-five acres. Vitanne Geneau, one of the house staff, was walking her horse down the road, its shoes pocking the dust and its tail switching. A breeze drove the clouds east over the mountain.

Weir was stockstill and scowling. "That mountain," he pointed, angry. All that rock looming over the estate, firred in purple, light and shadow played over it. A cloud lay riven at the peak like a gigged whale. He owned the damned thing. "What about it, Allston?"

He stared at me. "Nothing," he bowed his head. "Nothing."

I went for him at ten the next morning. He sat at the edge of the bed lacing his shoe. "So," he said. "Everyone's mustered."

"These people respect you, Mr. Weir. They understand and have nothing but best wishes for you. They have your best interests . . ."

"Then stop apologizing for them," he stood and stamped in the shoe. He did not want to hear anything about respect and heart. If he had to be introduced to his family and staff for the fourth time in his life he wanted to get on with it. He lifted his hand to the door and said with some resignation, "Lead." So we went down the staircase, through the sitting room and the library. He looked from side to side, memorizing his way through the atrium, past the pool. Celeste had assembled family and staff on the south lawn in two rows and he walked out that day, and stood with his hands in the pockets of his robe watching the grass sparkle, the foothills rolling west, perfect gardens on fire with wisteria and roses, the sunlight pouring over the dormers. Celeste dressed in a pale blue gown with a high neckline and pearls. On her left Bertrand itched around in a big blazer and red tie with his wooden gun in his pocket. He was trying not to laugh. Celeste pushed the boy's hand out of his mouth when Allston stepped ahead of me. She had a hard time displacing her look of impatience with Bert for a look of love for her husband. Nevertheless she tried. Her voice cracked with his name. "Good morning, Allston." She gave me a look that said this insipid formality, having a precedent in relapses three times, was stupid and did nothing but embarrass everyone. "Welcome home, darling," she stepped up and kissed his cheek. "We missed you. My name is Celeste. I am your wife. You can call me Celie." She offered up her cheek to be kissed but Weir didn't kiss it. Perhaps he did not believe that either. He took her hand and gave it a little heft.

"Celeste," he said. "Nice to meet you."

Bertrand stuck up his hand and said, "Bertrand Weir, sir. I am your son!" and he grinned, there being to his eyes no difference in his father but this game of cerebral possum he played now and then. Weir bent and put out his hand. The boy grabbed it in both his and squeezed with all his might.

And the staff. He met Crowell, his butler; Vitanne, his maid, again; Yetta and Sandra, downstairs domestics; Herman the groundskeeper; and Victor, chef. He met Albert Fournier, the lawyer and accountant who lived on the grounds and who had elected to wear a nametag on his lapel. Vitanne Geneau had come from Austria to study sculpture. She was nineteen, taller than six feet with a high waist and deep blue eyes, and in return for her education she served in Allston's household. Celeste was making plans to get rid of her.

Allston thanked everyone that morning and dismissed them. He walked back past the pool, through the atrium, the library and the sitting room, up the stairs and down the hall into his room and he shut the door. He opened the terrace doors and breathed in the cool air of the mountain, turning his memories over like dough in a cracked bowl. Crowell would tell me later that he rang down for every issue of *Artifact* ever published, blueprints of the house, a map of the estate, family photo albums and an accounting of every penny spent to maintain the house within the last month. He was not seen by anyone till Vitanne took him his lunch tray. When she entered the room and nodded, she sought his attention. She opened a small table by the velvet Queen Anne chair on the terrace and as Weir watched, she uncovered a lamb chop mornay and parslied potatoes, marinated carrots, a thick slice of Black Forest bread, a pewter butter tureen and a dish of baked eggs. She set a crystal cigarette holder on the table with a box of gold-tipped matches, and when she turned to leave she gave her master a strange nod.

He left his work and sat down and unfolded the linen. He looked up at the mountain and tasted the edge of the chop. It was rare and delicate. In his hands the silver felt heavy and old. The food was rich, and with each bite he closed his eyes and saw Jane hand the soup over. The stone house gathered around him with all the luxury built on the inspirations of visionary men and women. He was uneasy, and whispered to himself, "Probably never painted a picture worth a nickel." Then he remembered, as if by accident, the vase smashing between the feet of Christopher, the eyes of his daughter and the decrepit garden, sour celery and Sergeant Carey, the littered streets and Paley's torturous failures. He ate little, figuring these accretions on the life of Payofski must leave him inevitably as the result, Weir or not. He put down his fork, no longer hungry, and took up a cigarette and the matchbox.

Inside the matchbox he found a tiny piece of paper. Curious, he opened it and found a one-line note written in the hand of a schoolgirl: *Your diaries are safe.*

He lit the cigarette. The note he stared at a long time. He blew a smoke ring toward the mountain, which rode the still air like a halo of the truth. Home, was he? Not Payofski; not Paley. He lay his head back, Allston Weir (his face burned). A rich—a rich, respected man.

He would not tell me what he had been through or what was wrong, why he mistrusted us, why he slept behind a locked door, why his sudden, obsessive interest in Warren Paley's life and death. He spent those first weeks back puttering around the mansion in a smoking jacket, his slippers slapping the parquet, a teacup and saucer before him like a lantern, refusing to talk about anything. I asked everyone to keep an eye on him for it seemed to me there was a psychological component to this latest relapse, a sort of paranoia that went beyond the reactions of a man who'd had a gun put to his chest. Any second-year medical student could have told from the cut of his hair that he'd had brain scans. I could have telephoned around the Boston hospitals but each time I started it seemed an invasion of his privacy. The servants would encounter him at odd places in the house, reading *Artifact* or studying a picture. Yetta or Crowell surprised him; he would look embarrassed, but then remembering that he owned the house and paid for their services he would bark, "What are you staring at?" and go away, the cup chattering in the saucer.

Bertrand shadowed his father as often as he was allowed. He tagged along with his wooden gun and the deed to Procyon, watching his father rememorize the house and extend the radius of his knowledge. Sometimes they walked at the foot of the mountain or along the property line. Bertrand answered all the questions put to him by his father. The beech leaves were gilded copper and brass by then and the blue of the sky had deepened. Weir would look at his son with asperity for an honest answer to the questions; it gave the boy some authority to focus on and challenge, which he did by answering honestly and then laughing. By and by Weir would smile and take the boy's hand. Often they went to the stone bridge together and dropped bread to the fish wheeling in the cold water.

There were days he would talk only to Bertrand. The boy's deed to Procyon, by the way, was a present Weir had arranged for his sixth birthday. Outer space was the boy's chief interest and with some telephone calls to friends in Washington and Texas, and by the leverage of his influence, Allston got Bertrand title to a star in Canis Minor. Bertrand's ownership was legitimate. The title had come to him through the mail in copperplate on linen paper, officially notarized notwithstanding any search. Bertrand built a cosmogony all his own around Procyon, and for what it lacked in consistency, for all the lists of imaginary foes and allies kept changing and whether the atmosphere there was accommodating or fatal, he was king and commander in chief, honcho of a star that had nothing to do with this world where his father forgot his own identity and almost got assassinated for it. As he walked, Bertrand would pull out his wooden gun and shoot at this world—the world he perceived as threatening his father's life, and by extension his own.

But I was concerned those first weeks that Allston—that Mr. Weir—did not want to stay well. I say "stay"—tests of his amygdala were negative. I kept after him to tell me what treatment he had had. He sat there on the terrace in a cashmere sweater eating from a bowl of grapes and sliced orange, drinking a glass of Perrier and ignoring me.

"We should continue the treatments, whatever they were," I said. "It's important, Allston. You don't seem to understand the . . ."

"Don't tell me what's important," he said and looked up at me as if to say, "I know what you're up to and everybody else around here." Only he didn't say that, he said, "Let Celeste in on your way out and close the door from the other side." He was impossible, stubborn, rude. He had aged. It had been two weeks since the bullet wound healed but he acted as if it had carried a poison and if he didn't quite enjoy it, he was at least accommodating himself to it.

Celeste swept into the room that day with a flourish of black silk, a one-woman fete of self-regalia and perfect innocence. Her eyes were lined in magenta, there were pearls at her throat and bangles on her arms. Cirrus was piled high over the mountain and on the table by the Queen Anne chair was an issue of *Artifact*, a pen and the grapes he'd pick from and spit the seeds over the rail.

"Good morning, Allston," she breezed in. "Can we talk?"

"Please."

She leaned against the railing, blushing. "I won't take much of your time. I know how busy you are getting reacquainted. I wondered . . . I wondered if I could persuade you to cooperate more with Dr. Ames. He works awfully hard, and," she stepped up and put her hands on his shoulders, "we all care, for you. It seems you would, at least, be willing to do it for Bertrand. Talk to us, Allston. You remember what happened to you, Ames says. Boston was a part of your life. You've been home some weeks now and avoided all of us. Won't you share with us? You don't know how worried we were."

"I'm sorry I worried you," he peeled a grape.

"When you didn't call after six weeks I wanted to call the FBI. I was *sure* something was wrong. I was afraid . . ." He put another grape in his mouth, ". . . reporters," she turned away in pain. "You could have been kidnapped. I kept waiting for ransom calls. It was terrible," she turned, teary. Weir looked at her. He put his head over the railing and gave birth to the seed, watching it swerve in the updraft. "Celeste," he said, "you're my wife, but it seems we don't share a bed. Where do you sleep?"

"Pardon? Me?"

"I said I'm told you're my wife. Where do you sleep?"

"Why?"

"Why? Because I would like you to sleep with me. You're very lovely. Unless . . . did I ever abuse you? Did I ask you to sleep elsewhere?"

"No, not . . . in so many words."

"Then sleep with me. Tonight," he said, looking into her eyes. "Come to me."

"Allston, we haven't . . ." She wrung her hands.

"Since when?"

"Uh, oh . . . Nineteen- . . . You see," she turned, "we tried, but . . ."

"What?"

"You . . . ," she looked toward the mountain, "are impotent."

Allston sat back in the chair and nodded. Celeste could not face him. Both of them seemed to await some judgment to be delivered from the mountain. By and by Celeste glimpsed him in the corner of her eye, and turned and brightened, "Anyway. I thought we should make some arrangements, considering . . . The madness of the world these days. . . ."

"You must feel lonely."

"No one's being very nice to anyone. Kindness bores people nowadays . . . sincerity. They're *not* like us. It seems important that we finish the conversation you began the night before you left for California."

"Do you feel alone, Celeste?"

"You said," she turned her back on him, "you wanted the estate provided for in case you had a relapse," she lowered her head. "You wanted to make certain everyone was provided for in case you couldn't manage. We kept putting it off. It seemed inappropriate when you were healthy. We *do* love . . ." He had stood up. And he put his arms around her, but she went rigid and shoved him. She crossed her arms. Her look was icy.

Allston stood at arms' length. He looked down and sat back again in the chair. He stared at the mountain. "I'm sorry—you were saying?"

She sat at the table before him and crossed her legs. "You wanted Albert to look into arranging for the estate to be in my name. Do you remember?"

"Albert," he said, "Albert, Albert. That beetly fellow with the nametag."

"Yes, Allston."

"Yes," he looked away. "And how much is involved?"

"About ten million. I don't know. Not much liquid, perhaps three, although the notes . . . I mean—maybe two million." She leaned against the railing. "Mostly art property. Galleries, commissions. Albert has all the data." The sun was over the house. The shadows were long and Weir lifted a gold lighter from the table and a cigarette and he put his feet up on the rail, blowing the smoke east. Kept diaries, did he?

"Do you see that mountain?"

She looked at the cigarette, wondering why he had resumed that dirty habit, and at his feet cloddishly up on the rail.

"Recently I saw a painting of that mountain. Compared to the real thing, it was nothing."

"Beg pardon?"

"Nothing, I said. Hardware," he flicked ash. "A placemat," he smoked and picked a grape and peeled the skin and put the grape in his cheek. "Tell Mr. Fournier," he said, sucking, "to draw a will that preserves everything in your name, if anything happens to me. And I will look at it."

As Celeste stood Allston detonated the grape. She folded her hands, looking down at him, and blushed. A smile twitched at the corners of her mouth. "Everything. That would be best, Allston."

He waved his hand to mean that doing the best thing came naturally to him. But Celeste interpreted it as a dismissal and turned away from the terrace. Allston watched her as a naturalist might watch a butterfly he intended to trap in a cloud of ammonia, whose wings he would pin to the cork. "Celeste."

"Yes, darling?"

"I've looked through the catalog of the art in the house. It says we have three paintings by Warren Paley."

Celeste looked painfully at the mountain. "We may have had them thrown out," she said. "Bertrand had Crowell mail that hideous moon-horse to Warren's brother a couple of months ago. For some reason he was desperate for it."

"Tell Crowell to find what we have. Tell him to hang them in the hall near the study."

"Ally, you hated . . ."

He turned and glared at her. In the light of the room he suddenly saw Julie—the same eyes and the shape of her face. He saw the deceit too, with the difference that in his wife it looked cruel and self-assured whereas in his daughter he suspected doubt. I'm sure it was then that he realized fully what he had done and what had been done to him. It left him the victim of a burgeoning insanity and he could not conquer it by delivering himself of a confession to any of us. He didn't trust us. He could not lift the receiver to call Julie, to ask her why. He must have been more alone that day than ever in his life, and he told Celeste, "Just do it, please," and turned his back on her.

"Yes, Allston."

She left him, smiling. Crowell was activated. Crowell the butler was a man paid to have no opinions or definite presence, overtness of carriage or mien, no desires, no ideas. He was a function in a tailcoat. Only one original Paley was found in the house, a painting called *Five Squares*. Paley's signature slithered along the bottom of *Five Squares* like a garden snake. The painting hung that afternoon outside the study as though it had hung itself.

The next day Celeste warned me that Vitanne was trying to influence Allston against my medical advice and against Celeste herself. I didn't know where she got her information but I took it as truth and I took it personally. I found Vitanne in the paddock. When I told her she would be better off minding her own business, she drew herself up and stared as if I had called her a foul name. A breeze brought a curl of her hair down and her eyes flashed. Her horse bobbed its head once on her shoulder, but she didn't break the stare. She said, "You're only his doctor."

"That's right, Vitanne. If that's not reason enough I'm sure Mrs. Weir can think about your employment somewhere else. Or I might be able to find something amiss with your visa. You have no right to interfere with Mr. Weir's treatment."

She kept staring at me. I wondered if she would like to hit me. Her horse even leveled those big liquid eyes as if he knew I had threatened her. He whickered and blew. She turned and patted his throat but kept silent about my warning. She just looked as if I had slapped her and her eyes misted like a child about to say, "You don't fight fair." Fine—she would learn that if she had adult feelings for Allston Weir she had better have adult strategies. Everyone wanted something from Mr. Weir.

She turned and led the horse through the gate and past the trees. I walked back to the stable. Celeste whispered to me from a shadow. "Allston says," she hugged me from behind, "I should have Albert redraw the will as he sees fit."

"Come here," I pulled her out of the light. "As he sees fit, or you?"

"What's the difference?"

"He couldn't have meant it."

"Oh, now spoil it."

I shook my head. Allston was spotting her some advantage and she didn't know it. It was as if she forgot. Her eyes were big in the smell of tack and provender; she opened her palm on my groin. "You seem to have a loose part here, Doctor. Shall I tighten it for you?"

I glanced out at the maid spurring the stallion across the meadow, her hair flying back like an Amazon.

"Don't underestimate him, Celie—or your little maid's second sense. I mean it. She watches you."

"Let her. I'll fire her," she shook her head. "I don't love Allston, and as for you . . . you, Doctor, I hate." She pressed her hand against me. I tugged the waist of her pants and said, "Pretend. Try to. Your husband's ill, not stupid."

"Smile when you swear at me," she pulled me back into a stall. The cool air breathed in the leather and straw and the blankets where she lay back and pulled me down.

"Pretend, Celeste."

"Take me," she tugged the belt of her trousers and pulled my hand down. "*Make* love." So she acted twenty, knowing I could not resist those silk trousers coming down and the horses pawing the dirt in the stable. "You're not much of a liar," I said. She pulled me on and winced. "It's," she said, "ah just oh God. As you say we . . . have . . . one lie for . . . everyone . . . we meet, oh Christ Fos . . . ter!" I pushed her back. "He won't," she whispered, "get better!" she said. Yes—she meant it, too. I had had Celeste in the stables, the meadow, on the shore of the lake, in her brass bed, in my car. I'd had her as an intact nymphet of sixteen and every year after. I liked the torment on her face when we made love. I liked making love to a woman who thrived on appearances, who worshiped surfaces. It was so interesting to get to the bottom of all the affectation. I didn't love Celeste in the classical sense, by which I mean the romantic sense. She didn't want love in the romantic sense. She wanted to be fucked and bitten and reminded of what she was.

The following day I had to tell Allston that if he wouldn't share facts about his treatment in Boston he would most likely get sick again; in other words he would forget everything. When I told him this he smiled. He smiled and thanked me and told me to go tend to my other patients. "If you don't have any other patients," he said, "go make some." (He had not lost his touch.) Late that afternoon he put on a coat and headed up the mountain on foot "for recreation." The fall light glowed in the trees. It was not cold enough for gloves but his breath was visible. Beyond the meadow and back into the woods the trail steepened. At places he grabbed branches and roots to pull himself above the trees to the rock ledge where he could look down at everything, his face strained, his breath heavy, his hands in his pockets like a general. The house spread out below like a fortress. The wind blew down from the mountain like the breath of whatever god could return him a relapse for the pain of being unable to forget his existence as Payofski or Paley. He owned it, he knew, he owned everything by the inspirations of madmen who understood the kinship between light and consciousness. Yet he had done those artists well too. He had made them rich. He turned and mounted the trail. As he walked he felt the thorn in his soul, the damnable barb of his incest. Not long after he broke through the woods on the tarn and stood on the shore, walking along it until he found the second path leading to the bower. He pushed his way through to a fallen pine tree and sat there, absolutely still.

Five minutes later he heard the horse. Through a break in the trees he saw its tail flying back, Vitanne bent to the mane, flying up. The ground

Payofski's Dyscovery [65]

trembled and the horse briefly disappeared, then reappeared, its head long and determined. The ground thundered closer. Allston stood and faced the clearing. In time the bower shivered and opened and the horse ducked under the trees, its noble head bowed as Vitanne, high on the nineteen hands, bent to his throat and guided him in with a whisper. She dismounted, her hair blown wild and her shirt crisp and white and rising, her eyes as blue as an ocean. She smiled at her master, then bent and extracted the envelope from her boot, all without a word.

Allston took it from her and tore it open.

Vitanne Geneau. You will remind me where I hid my diaries in case I have a relapse. Under no circumstances will you tell Mrs. Weir that they exist.

The note was in his handwriting. "So," he looked up. "You're with me?"

She took the note back and pushed the envelope down in her boot. She straightened and swept her hair back. "You keep them in a box, Mr. Weir. Over here." She walked through the clearing and bent to the fallen tree. She brought the box out of the bole and handed it to him, staring at his eyes. Her horse bobbed and she patted his throat, speaking softly to him in German. The box was heavy and rusted. It contained his memory, his history, or such as it was, himself.

"How many times have you shown me that letter?" he asked.

"This is the second time."

The breeze came up through the bower. He stared at her and she at him, waiting, he thought, he did not know for what. What did she want? What did he hope to learn?

"Vitanne . . ." he looked down at the box.

"She doesn't love you, sir. She can't."

"No. She doesn't love anyone."

"Not the way I . . ."

"Vitanne." His voice was curt and Vitanne blushed again, looking down. "Forgive me. Please."

He kept looking down at the box, weighing it. When he looked up again Vitanne was mounting the stallion, looking down at him sadly, as if it was the last time she would ever see him or have half a chance. He stepped up and held the horse's bit.

"Vitanne, I have a daughter, Julie." He stopped.

She looked down at him.

"That is who I meant, Mr. Weir," she said, and she pulled the horse's head around. Weir let the bit go and she clucked him through the trees, then she spurred him and they thundered again, the dirt rolling like a war drum and her figure immobile over the bounding horse, her hair blown back in the storm. . . .

It was to that bower on the mountain where he went every day after— up the trail, fighting for his breath to the box, more and more afraid that someone would find it, that one day it would be gone or that Vitanne would betray him too. Celeste wasted no time outlining Albert Fournier's duty in terms of the estate. She had a couple of men brought in, experts in executing exchanges of vast amounts of money under venal circumstances. The three of them were standing around a silver teacart in the atrium when Celeste said, "Gentlemen," and pressed her hands under her chin, her shoulders drawn together in a pose of misgiving. "As you know Mr. Weir has not been well these years. I want to assure you that this redrawing of the will has his blessing . . ." And she went on, masterful—her fey glances hinting that more than gyracinguloplasticchoreosis was wrong with him, that Allston Weir was not entirely sane. She played those men like a stripper undulating out of restraint, out of doubt, enveloping the three in veiled truths and the promise of a hefty fee. The sun struck the teacart and bathed the men in vibrant light. They watched her as she spoke and moved in a way that appealed to certain drab fantasies they felt with respect to her body. Celeste could be slippery, and they sipped tea and said, "Sorry to hear it, Mrs. Weir . . . sorry . . . sorry . . . if there's anything else . . ." She tipped her head to Mr. Fournier and stared long enough to rid him of any idea that a redrawing would need Allston's signature, for she had certain medical affidavits that could be produced at the snap of a finger. Albert Fournier was a man she could have swallowed alive in one of her sensual looks; he would have come out nothing but bones and feathers. So she put him in charge.

And it began that Allston's will was brought out and examined and for whatever reasons I did not discourage it. Fournier and his men were given desks in the atrium with the beautiful view south from the poolside and a button to push for tea and supper. Each man had a computer in a suitcase and Fournier an IBM he set up like a field telephone in a military siege. Meanwhile Allston was montane, looking down with his box, aware that the lights burning in the west wing meant the evaporation of his wealth and maybe he didn't give a damn. I was sure he would wait to do anything about it till he had something ironclad. Unfortunately I could not convince Celeste that loss of memory was not synonymous with ignorance.

The diaries he found in the steel box had cracked leather bindings. The pages were yellow. I'm sure that as he held them he would not have traded them for the Holy Grail or anything. He might have even killed for them. He opened them and searched out any mention of Paley and Paley's wife, his daughter, then he squinted with a hunger and followed the lines of his cramped writing with a finger.

> Another rambling letter from Warren. He is bent on depriving me of her—says it's the only way to purify her of her upbringing. Apparently he thinks I was a bad father; odd considering that he abuses her and I never laid a finger on her in my life. I know he hits her. He drinks and gets carried away with some vengeance he has. When I ask her why she stays with him, she says she loves him. Of course that's the end of the discussion because I can't reasonably accuse her of lying. Or she smarts back, "Why do you stay with Celeste?" Trying to show her there is a difference seems pointless. The more I ask her to leave him and come home, the more she considers loving him some private exaltation or else she wants to punish me for something. The way she looks at me, she smiles when I get angry. Sometimes it seems she thinks there's a competition between Warren and me for her affection. She seems to forget that I am her father and could not love her that way. I do sometimes wish that painter didn't exist . . .

He went up there in any weather. Bundled in a lodencoat, a karakul hat, big leather hiking boots and kid gloves, he opened the books to the rain, the fog, the haze and the truth of a past often repeated. He sat on the fallen tree, his estate spread before him in the valley like a Thanksgiving table full of plastic food, the blustery sky churning whitecaps in the tarn and river.

> . . . Paley's asinine belief he doesn't have to be democratic. He doesn't have to be a gentleman. What kind of position is this for a man who wants acknowledgment for his work? He's so stubborn and cruel, even if I liked his work I would be disinclined to help him. Advance the career of the man who terrorizes my daughter and threatens me. Does she want to punish me or herself or both of us? What does she want? She tempts me, flirts with me. It's not my imagination. She's accidentally let me see her naked then apologizes, but it's transparent. What does she expect? She's a beautiful

girl—her body would tempt any man in that way. Why she picked this nutty painter with the ego will always bewilder me. . . .

He has no manners. His hair and neck are dirty and it kills me to think she could ever compare us as men. He has the eyes and vanity of a starving hawk and he smokes like the Ruhr. I can't figure him out and he gives me nothing to go on. He wants me to spend time parsing his abstractions. He seems to think I am the man who should help him. She says he's too proud to sell on the sidewalk or vanity galleries, a price better artists than he have paid. If I can't respect him it would be hypocrisy to respect his work. Yet I'm pigheaded, he says. The last time he fell apart I met her for lunch at the hospital and gave her a thousand. I was sure she looked at me as if she would divorce him if only there were someone to take up the slack in her life, to check the loneliness. Me? I didn't mention it. I kissed her and left and thought about it all the way home. Can't remember driving, just this insane fantasy . . . Me?

There was a storm coming, a blanket of dark clouds traveling on the edge of the light. It began to drizzle. Weir looked down, his finger frozen on the page. She had made a fool of him. Paley had turned the tables on a man who dissembled his lust for his own daughter on rejections on principle, on artistic ideals, personal integrity and the false belief that art had to fit within certain confines. Weir's face burned. Shame had never been a familiar emotion before Washington Street, but reading these thoughts now, in his diary, he was ashamed. Raindrops pattered through the leaves and fell on the page.

Phone call May 16. Warren has stumbled again. Julie sounded scared and exhausted. I went down under the pretense of a trip to the MFA. The thing is I'm afraid Warren is not very resilient for this life he has chosen. He intends always to innovate and works at the cutting edge of his sanity and then loses it. I picked her up for a ride to the hospital. She said he had overdone the prescription drugs and started storming around, lighting candles, drawing the shades at midday. Demanded silence. He's at McLean now. Apparently broke three windows and threw a chair down on the street to stop the noise. Broke some glasses and put his fist through the wall. More than a hundred stitches for his forearm. Julie didn't know who would pay for the ambulance. He hit her on the left side of the head; she says it was an accident, only a concussion, and that she should have stayed out of his way. I have no doubts that that man will kill himself one day. Can only pray he doesn't take anyone with him. "How's Celeste?" Julie smiled. Says I have prevented Warren's success by turning over all his slide submissions to the board at *Artifact*. Obviously my opinion of his work is biased

Payofski's Dyscovery [69]

when he begins clubbing my daughter in the head. He's suffered so, she says. Is that why you love him? Who does she think I am? My blood boiled. I pulled over and kissed her, but had to push her away. What was I doing? I kissed her! I wanted her, she wanted me! . . .

That night he came down the mountain in the rain. He was pale and the thunder rolled. There was a light on in the library and he was spoiling for a fight. But it was only Bertrand in the library, coloring the library floor.

"Where's Celeste?" Weir said.

The boy looked up. "In the pool," he turned to his colorbox. "With the spies."

Weir left the library and went down the hall to the west wing, walking like a machine. He shoved through the double doors to the atrium and stared down the length of the pool at the accountants in the foliage, and his wife up on the mirador like Isis. The mechanical men looked up at him. They blanched with the complexion of thieves and Weir looked at them, at the sleeping pool, at the rain pattering the glass. His hair and coat were soaked. The accountants looked from him to Celeste to see if it was a mistake to think he was already insane.

"Darling?" Celeste said, "What is it?" her voice tender, echoing. "Are you all right? Do you want me to call the doctor?"

"About two months ago," Weir said, "Warren Paley sent me a painting, and a cassette tape I was to open in the event of his death." His voice echoed around the tiles and pool. "Where are they?"

"Tape?" She glanced at Mr. Fournier.

Weir walked around the pool. He raised his diary high in his hand.

"He mailed a painting, a self-portrait, and a cassette tape, Celeste. Warren Paley, our son-in-law. He wanted me to keep them for him in case something happened. And something did. Now where are they?"

"I think you may have had them thrown out."

"No, don't lie to me. I would not throw out a man's last painting or his death letter, no matter what I thought of him personally. Besides I never throw anything out. It's right here," he opened the book. "February 3. 'You never throw anything out.' Now you tell me where they are."

"You said, Allston," the accountants looked from him to her, "you said, never to mention his name in this house. When he was here last you almost shot him. We agreed on this. Isn't that right, Mr. Fournier?"

"In fact, sir, I was just revising your will with this wonderful machine you bought for me," said Fournier. "Observe," he shot his cuffs. "With two keystrokes I can globally delete the names of Julie and Warren Paley from your will—abinga, abanga—done! Erased!"

Celeste stepped up quickly. "What do you think I would do with his painting and his tape, Allston? I had Crowell throw them out."

"When!"

The accountants jumped like machines plugged into the same switch.

"I don't remember!"

"Crowell!" Weir yelled. The name ricocheted. Before long the butler appeared in the Dutch doors facing the pool, looking immaculate.

"Sir?"

"A cassette tape from Boston, two months ago. Addressed to me. Warren Paley addressed it. Where is it?"

"Pitched, sir. Just yesterday."

"Where?"

"The landfill, sir. The main ditch."

"Bring a car around."

"Sir."

"Allston?" Celeste said. "Now, dear, you can't go to the landfill on a night like this. Crowell? Mr. Fournier? Perhaps if you pushed that little button, we could get the doctor . . ."

"Let me," Weir said, and with no blood in his face he walked around the pool to Mr. Fournier's desk and ripped the button out of the wall. He leaned down to Mr. Fournier and whispered, "*Like* global deletion, do you, Mr. Fournier?" and when he stood up he had the monitor of the computer in his hands. He spun half around and flung it at the pool. The sleeping water exploded. The keyboard trailed from the coiled cord like a whelp, crashing from the desk and diving in the pool too.

Mr. Fournier stood, crushed, clutching his vest as the waves curled toward the tiles.

"Allston!" Celeste screamed. "The *misery* she caused us!"

"Where's the damned landfill?" he started to storm out.

"All her life, she *humiliated* us!"

Mr. Fournier stood poolside and stared down. Weir turned and stabbed a finger.

"Julie is more my wife right now than you are! No man in his right mind would marry you, not as Payofski, Mozart, Daffy Duck or Adolf Hitler! And as for you, Mr. Fournier. As soon as you fish out that electronic abacus, you can globally delete *her*!"

"You're mad!"

Fournier whimpered and threw himself in.

"Someone call an ambulance! Call Dr. Ames! Hurry!"

"Touch that phone, I'll rip out your spinal cord and strangle you with it! Better yet I'll shoot you! I have a gun, don't I?" the blood rushed back to his face. "*Crowell!*"

"Here, sir."

"Get my goddam gun so I can shoot somebody!"

"Sir."

"Crowell, *no!*" Celeste reached toward him. Weir stormed out of the atrium and down the hall. By the time he gained the front door the Jaguar was purring in the porte cochère and the rain was snow. He jumped off the porch and jerked the driver out of the front seat and yelled, "What are you doing in my car! Who the hell are you!"

"Alexander, sir. Your driver. And may I say what a pleasure it is once again to meet . . ."

"Where's the landfill!"

"Five miles south, on this road, sir. There's a fence. Crack your window. You can't miss it. Sir."

Allston jumped in the car, stripped two gears and burned out of the gate. By the time Celeste phoned me it took ten minutes to cut through her hysterics to find out Allston was hellbent for the dump and raving mad over some damn painting. I asked her why she had thrown the thing out and she said, "What's the difference!" and slammed the phone down. She was worried that he was going out there and everybody was going to know about it. The ladies who liked to debunk her would have a field day. I dressed and went for her—forty-five minutes through the wet snow. It was almost dark when she got in the front seat and said, "The landfill," wearing a scarf and dark glasses, utterly disgusted. The sun was setting. The landfill was in a cirque on the north side of the mountain. On our way she explained Weir's "fit" and said he had tried to drown Mr. Fournier. I thought that at least Allston would be alone . . .

No—wrong. When we got there the sun was glowing scarlet in a gash of low clouds. The landfill was a string of gravel and trash hills on a dirt plain surrounded by fence. But there were nine or ten cars parked along that fence. Young people, shadows wandering like bodies lost and searching the ground for their souls, wandered, bending, searching for Paley's self-portrait. Parked at the end of the cars were two black-and-whites with five cops looking things over, the blue light spirling on the smoke and the fires that burned in fissures. The fires glowed against the black and red sky and the kids eyed the police and picked their way.

What a mess. I got out of the car and walked up to the police. They were watching the trespassers as if trying to decide what it meant or how to approach it. "Officer," I said. "You know who that man up there is?" Weir was standing high on one mound supervising, yelling down at the kids like Moses.

"Who wants to know?" the cop asked.

"His doctor," I said, bringing out the syringe I carried and a sedative. You could hear Weir yelling, "Look over there! You, with the headphones, circle wider!" The cop looked at me and shrugged. "His name is Allston Weir," I said. "He's not well. That's his wife in my car, over there. You understand the embarrassment this could cause? You are Officer . . ."

The cop looked at the needle, up at Weir against the bloody sky, and at the little fires. "Come on," he said. "What's he doing up there, anyway?"

"None of your business."

One other cop followed us around the flat side of the fill. It was a steppe of trash that gave under your feet and the snow glazed it. These kids Weir had enlisted were bent at the waist like sowers and he entreated them, offering ten thousand dollars to the one who found the painting and tape. He'd throw his arms out and yell ten grand and the teenagers snooped with a frenzy, picking up and discarding, picking up, discarding. The little fires burned like something out of prehistory, the smoke threading out of the earth and rising through the snow to the sunset. When we got to the base of the mound I yelled, "Allston!" and sent one cop around the other side.

Weir looked down at me and swore. He lifted his arms against the wounded sky and yelled, "Unless you're here to help, Ames, clear out! We don't need you!"

"I am here to help!" I yelled. "Hang on!"

"Then get out there and search for that painting! You don't know her!"

I had no idea what he meant. He was yelling at the kids, "You!"

again. "Farther along the edge of the ditch! Look in that heap over there!" and a couple of kids with beer cans ran to where he pointed and searched like hell. "We're coming up, Allston!" I yelled, and filled the hypodermic, nodding to the cop. Weir would not give up without a fight, that was certain. He would not come down with us begging, we would have to go after him. As we started in, I saw the van coming down the road. It was what I was afraid of—a television crew. It crawled down the link fence and stopped and two men began unloading cameras from the back. I nudged the cop. "Can you stop them?" He turned and yelled at three officers who were trying to chase the kids out. "No pictures!"

"I'm coming up, Allston!"

"Try, you frigging quack!"

I held the needle up and planted my foot on the heap. It had a skin of wet papers and cans and snow-diapered cellophane. Trying to walk on it you bent and dipped, twisting like a building in a hurricane. I had to support my weight with my fingers spread and the needle raised like a rifle. The officer with me was having no better a time. He slipped and swore and turned his nose up. The cop around the back was having an easier time—no snow on that side. Every now and then I would look up to mark our way and see Weir's athletic form steadied with one foot up on some kind of drum, squinting through the snow at the kids and the search patterns.

The cops at the fence were heading off the camera crew, but a man with a camera on his shoulder was shooting from the distance. In the car Celeste had shrunk to almost nothing.

"Allston!" I yelled. "They're trying to take your picture! Do you know what that means?"

"Ten thousand dollars, you idiot!" he shouted. "Don't just stand there! There's a Paley somewhere in this slag heap worth ten times that!"

So, he was doing this for Paley, but he hated Paley. I crept up a little higher. I slipped on some bottles and a little fabric of snow fell away and revealed a fire, trash burning deep in the mound like a boil. Sidestepping it I gauged I could reach him in three more steps, which I tried to take at a run, and then slipped at his feet. He grabbed me and hauled me upright.

"Allston!"

He hauled my face into his.

"I loved her!" he spat at me. "I fell in love with her!"

"Allston, let me breathe!"

The cop who scaled the back side made it over and lunged at him. He grabbed his knees at the same time the officer who had followed me lunged and grabbed him. The result was that Weir didn't move. The cops struggled, puzzled and slipping.

"I made love to her!"

"What are you talking about!"

"Julie, you ass! My daughter!"

Below the kids had paused to look up and see if the reward was still in force. The camera crew tried to make an end run of the fence and the police were chasing them. They were trying to film on the run. I was slipping meanwhile, strangling in Weir's fist.

"It doesn't matter, Ally! Listen to me! Paley's dead!"

"He isn't!"

"He killed himself!"

"He's alive!"

"He was a bastard! You despised him! You had a right!"

"He had genius! I destroyed it!"

"He was a fool, Allston!" I glanced at the needle. "He was a savage! He abused Julie!"

"He was my son-in-law!"

The three of us wrestled with Allston like crabs trying to pin down a piling. The youngsters on the plain were running out of the grip of the cops when the cameraman bolted by and slipped and fell across a burning tire. He started to scream. The officer who had been chasing him dived on him and put him out and smashed the camera at the same time. Too bad. On top of that stinking heap the four of us swayed, the snow blowing in our eyes, Allston raving mad and strong as a bull. Finally I got a grip on the needle and jabbed it through his shirt. The effect seemed to take forever. I threw the needle down and his hand came up, the finger crooked as in paintings of the Assumption. Before long he grew weaker and squinted. His grip on my throat relaxed and I tore his hand away and fell backward. The next thing I knew the loss of tension on this side caused him to sway and the rest of them came tumbling down after me, Weir and the two officers sliding down on their butts first, then head over heels. When I looked up, Weir was standing, covered in snow and papers, stumbling, swaying. I was dizzy, flattened. The dose I gave him should have knocked out a man three times his size, but he turned to the bloody sunset, the police, and he grabbed me around the throat and stood me up again, and he hissed at me, "You're fired, Ames."

"Julie was vicious! She used your love against you and against everyone!"

"She had her reasons!" he shook me.

"What? She flirted with you when she was old enough to know the difference! She wanted you on her side against her mother! She tried to kiss you on the mouth!"

Slowly his eyes closed and he jerked them open. They closed again. He tried to focus on me. "You're fired, Ames." His hand fell away. "Catch him," I said. As he fell into the arms of the police a young man came running across the fires, his voice shrill. "Mr. Weir! The tape from Boston!" He was running fast with a cop in hot pursuit. The boy dodged his way toward us, the tape held high. He turned and kicked the cop between the legs and the other kids tore after him too.

Bertrand Draws a Bead on the Age of Enlightenment

I remember when Julie was little she and Allston had a game. Before her bedtime Weir spread his feet and she sat on his shoe, straddling it, her arms wrapped around his calf. When she said go, Weir went striding around the house and Julie squealed and ordered him to take this or that direction, to growl like a giant or step higher or faster. Hay foot straw foot she turned her face up screaming in laughter as he looked down; he took his giant swing steps with her riding on his shoe. That should have seemed more innocent to me than it did.

He had pictures of her at age twelve and thirteen when they went iceboating. He used to carry the pictures in his suit. The hard ice and wind whipped red into their faces and brought tears from the flight of the boat. Wrapping her face in a hat, Weir plied the sheet and steered the blade, watching the grape-colored sky cloud over. The boat skidded across the lake, carving the ice and spewing frost, heeling as they flew. Julie sat between his legs and as it got colder and faster she hunkered and he pulled her close. When they went too fast and heeled too far she shut her eyes. She burrowed into his lap holding the hot chocolate thermos and looked up at him. He worked the sheet around from one tack to another and now and then she opened her eyes, burrowed deep between his legs and closed them again as the boat flew back and forth, tipping in the wind and ice.

I took his pulse as he slept. It was not that his daughter could never do wrong in his eyes. Though he never hit her he could get angry. There was the time she was fourteen, she jumped in the BMW and headed for New York. Around Troy she hit speeds of 85 miles an hour before the state police pulled her over and brought her back. She was put to bed. Allston fumed. For a week he thought of her in that flying machine and had nightmares of losing her. At about that time she began sleepwalking and went to her mother one night at three a.m. and slapped her across the face. I started her on Dilantin.

Now as for Paley, since he was dead I had no problem faulting him for his part. He was more insane than not. I'd known him better than I cared to. He drank and got mad ideas—rituals. For a year he would only paint by candlelight. He decided sunlight was bad, a deception. All his stuff that year came out haloed and dark, portraits in purple and brown. I think Warren clung to a belief he could influence his world by abusing Julie and I could see no valid reason, looking at Allston's still face, why he should feel guilt for Warren Paley's death. That death had taken a burden off us as far as I was concerned. He was not to be understood.

When Julie was sixteen and swam at the lake that should have seemed innocent. Her suit was white—two strands of fabric so narrow you could almost see the electrons. Local boys came out of the woods around the lake and chased her. Their randy laughter echoed in the valley. For refuge she ran away, screaming, into her father's arms and he would sweep her up, covering her with his shoulders and back, bent over the lounge chair, hiding her as the boys threw buckets of cold water and begged him to let her go. She loved to wrestle; Weir would cover her and tickle her as she arched her back and he blew on her belly and she screamed not to be given away, unmindful that one of her little breasts had slipped the glossy triangle and awakened under her father's chin. It did seem to me that as she became a woman, the more Allston tried to push her away as a man, the closer she came to him. And when she married Paley, when she was twenty, I think Allston's whole life, the whole direction of his life, fell under a cold and jealous shadow.

The sedative wore off around midnight. Allston sat up in the dark and remembered the landfill, his diaries, the fiasco on the mound, the lost painting—the memories limped toward him in his mind like beggars— and pulling on a robe he left the gold room for water, his eyes ringed in sleep. At the landing he looked downstairs at the light in the drawing room. He forgot his thirst when he saw Bertrand skulking in the downstairs hall, eavesdropping.

In the drawing room Celeste whispered to me, "He *made love* to her?

Do you know if that got out . . . . Year after year he forbids even mention of her name in this house. And then he sneaks off and has *relations* with her?"

I poured some Napoleon into a snifter. "You're exaggerating," I said, slumped in the chair. "He couldn't have meant 'made love' in that sense."

"Oh," she tucked her feet under her, "you're so cool and loyal."

"Yes, for one thing nobody will believe it even if he did. And for another thing, what if he did?"

"My husband—an incestuous paranoid."

"Why don't you admit to yourself you never understood him," I said. "Not when he was healthy and building his life, not now that he's sick with a disease that doesn't show. On the surface."

"Don't preach to me."

"All right, divorce him. You'll lose. He's beginning to remember."

"Why shouldn't I? I have the right. He's incapable of managing his affairs."

"You mean his money, so divorce him. What's wounded is your pride . . ." and to hell with it. She stared from the light of the lamp, her nose a shadow across her cheek.

"Our position . . . ," she said.

"Our position is a function of his. I was downwind of him, remember? I don't smell like a rose and neither do you. And if you have delusions about his incest, as you call it, get them out of your mind before morning. I intend to tell him about us." I sipped the brandy. After a minute she said, "Crowell!" and that name, being round like a marble, rolled through the house and fetched up the ears of the butler. He appeared in the door in his livery and said, "Madam?"

"Take Dr. Ames's shoes and have them cleaned."

He came in and went away with my shoes.

"You're not . . . ," she said.

"I am. You know the funny thing is she always did seem to be in love with him. When you think back. Think back, Celeste; it's a gift. There was something between them even when she tried her best to make him mad. Remember when she burned the iceboat? Burned it in the middle of the lake. Nothing left but the bow runner and a hole in the ice and the mast sticking up. She came back stinking of gasoline and guilt, and what did he do? Went out and bought a new one." The art of money.

Celeste rose. "How can you smile in the face of this?" Her shadow fell in the hall. "She used to want him to do that disgusting thing, that blowing on her belly. We should . . . ," she stopped pacing and faced the hallway. "Bertrand!" she barked. "Bertrand, come in here!"

Almost half a minute passed. The boy skulked around the door. He wore his sportcoat and looked between Celeste and me as if we wove judgments that his feelings and intelligence couldn't influence.

"How many times have I told you not to spy?"

"I wasn't. Spying."

She stood right over him. He didn't seem to know if the stream of words about to shower down would scald him or leave him frozen in his tracks. He looked down at the carpet, his lower lip puffed out.

"Is Julie here?"

"Now what gave you that idea? You are to forget Julie. How many times have I told you?"

He pointed across the room. "That's Daddy's"—the package with the tape. "You magnetized it." He pulled out his gun and shot me. "Pkiiuee!"

The brandy swirled. "Good shot, Bert."

"Don't point that dirty thing at the doctor."

He backed up a step. "Daddy saw Julie. Julie can come to Procyon with Daddy, but not you!" he pointed.

"Why not me?"

"You do shots!" he said. "On Procyon the wolfcrows . . ."

"Good for them."

"Go to bed, Bertrand."

"We're going to Procyon with Vitanne. Julie can come. Death to poopy liars!"

"Bertrand!"

"You put Daddy to sleep and killed Julie!" he ran over to the sideboard and grabbed the tape and Allston's diary and bolted, shooting up the room, "Pkieeu! Pkieeu!"

Celeste sighed and studied the shadows where he went as if they symbolized the disreputable blackness of her life. It seemed her mind shifted away from the boy finally or that he had never been in the room. She looked at me, shaking her head. "All this *shit* about Procyon . . ."

"He's hyperactive," I said. "Put a little coffee in his milk tomorrow, see if it helps." He had built this whole damn thing around being president of Procyon. We discussed it for a minute, Celeste and I, and Bertrand stole upstairs with the tape. He sneaked down to his father's door and listened. As I climbed the stairs he pushed his way in and closed the door behind him.

Weir was drinking water on the terrace. He heard the pop of Bertrand's salute hand to thigh and turned around. In the light of his big, serious face the boy seemed to forget everything. He walked in and carefully put the tape and diary at the edge of the bed. Weir watched him and looked down and saw that the boy's sportcoat hung down in his palms and his trousers broke heavily over his shoes. His shoelaces were double-knotted. The collar of his shirt hung so loose the points could have been epaulets for a size twelve service cap.

Allston left the terrace and stood over the bed and over Bertrand.

"Who buys your clothes, young man?"

The boy looked down and up.

"Mummy does."

"Why don't you roll up the sleeves of your coat?" Weir pointed. "There's more shoulder in that blazer than you'll need in a year. Come here." Weir stooped, his knees cracking; he grabbed a handful of the coat behind Bertrand and took it in till it hung within reason.

"How is that?"

"Good," the boy said.

"Yes," Weir stood, and looked down at his son. "How old are you again?"

"Seven."

"And what kind of tie is that? What's the red stuff?"

Bertrand stood enthralled by his father's voice. "Wolftrawlers," he whispered. "Vitanne made it."

"Ah, Procyon," Weir said, and he extended his hand. "Come out here and show me which one of those lights up there is Procyon."

They walked out to the terrace together. The clouds had divided. The sky was a black beach of stars over the white lawn and Bertrand looked up at the heavens, and from the heavens to his father, who said, "Which one?"

The boy said, cocking his head as if applying the sense of sight to the verifiability of Procyon broke every law of reason, "There," and pointed up. "That little one on the outside of those big ones."

Weir scowled upward. "The one on the rim of that white splotch?"

"No, the other one. On that side, see? By the two medium ones with the light between."

"The one right over my thumb," Weir put his hand up. "It's in a triangle of two medium ones and that huge red one."

"No."

"No?"

"No. The one on top of that . . . square, that looks like a round thing but bigger. Right over my thumb." He put his hand up like his father, squinting. "See it?"

"No."

"No?"

"No."

Bertrand looked at his father with grave disappointment. Weir said, "You're kind of young to be president, anyway."

"I'm the oldest one," he said and turned from the terrace and ran full-speed and dived onto his father's bed. His father stepped back in the room. The boy looked up at him sideways.

"Mummy said you loved Julie."

Weir stared. It seemed he was looking at Bertrand but he was not, and then he cleared his throat and he was. "What do you know about Julie, Bertrand? Do you love her? Do you miss her?"

The boy nodded.

"When was the last time you saw her?"

"She came with Warren. Who painted the horse and went mad, like Grampa," he looked down. It was written in the bedspread. "He yelled and she went upstairs. So he yelled. He punched her. You said . . . and you yelled but. He threw something down the stairs, and yelled, 'Crowell you limey cocksucker! Get my car,' and Mummy . . . Julie cried. But you," he lifted his arm and brought it down in a sweep across his face, "said go away. And never come back here. Because you're not a *Weir* anymore."

Weir turned, hands clasped behind him, and looked out at the stars and the snow and the mountain.

"Did Julie yell at any time?"

"No. She cried."

"Did you tell her you loved her when she was here?"

Bert did not seem to want to answer. Allston turned back and found him nodding, picking at the bedspread.

"Then it was Mr. Paley who got mad first?"

"Yes. He looked like this." He stuck out his tongue, pulled his cheeks out and made wild eyes. "Except his hair was like a woman's."

"Did you like him?"

"No!"

"Why not? Because I didn't like him?"

Bert was silent.

"Julie loved him," Allston said.

The boy ran out to the terrace and grabbed the railing and hung there. Then he stood and came back, his hands behind him.

"Nope. She didn't."

"What, nope. She married the man. Tell the truth."

"It was a lie. Like Dr. Ames and Mummy."

Allston stared again from his son outside at the mountain. He was getting to the bottom of something in his life, independent of his name and a formal identity. He was on the track of something deeper when suddenly the chase ended. He had taken a wrong turn. Why . . . ? It would have been something no maid could remind him of, and he looked at the tape at the edge of the bed pensively, and the diary and said, "Thank you for the tape, Bertrand." He went to it and picked it up. "You need . . . ," he said.

"What?"

Weir looked down.

"Clothes that fit."

Bert looked down too, prepared to be ashamed if that was the object of the question. But his father was smiling and he sat on the bed. He put his hands on the boy's shoulders and looked him in the eye.

"Do you love your father?"

"Yes."

"Why? He goes away. When he comes back he forgets your name and how old you are. He tells your sister to go away and stay away. Now, how . . ."

" 'Cause I want to." The boy unscrewed himself from Weir's grip in time to see a brace of wolfcrows drop to the terrace, burning the wrought iron and melting the brick, turning the snow to water in a flood arching over the mountain, spilling over the house in a wave. He ran out and buried his face in the velvet chair. To Weir it was portentous and unnerving. His heart skipped a beat as he walked out and gathered Bertrand up and brought him back to the bed. He wondered what he had done in the past to stop the crying, what he had ever said, what he had known about the boy's feelings. Ten thousand if you'll stop crying, Bert. He held him to his chest quietly, rocking him. "I'm going to bring Julie back home, Bertrand."

Bertrand sobbed. His father held him until such time as the boy could look out and find the terrace was a terrace, and there was snow on the grass and the universe was in order. Finding his world thus Bert said, "Ask more love questions," and wiped his sleeve across his eyes. "Do you love Julie?"

"Yes, Bertrand. I do. I did a bad thing."

"What?"

"I made Julie do a bad thing."

"What?"

"I," Weir said, "made her let me make her do a bad thing." He drew the boy close. One day Bertrand would understand what had befallen the family and rotted it. If in the future it could be proved that he had willed his sickness, Allston wanted Bertrand to understand that, too, and preserve the memory of his father. It was a lot to ask but he knew—Bertrand would know—that the only thing a man like his father could do, a proud man who could not lead the life of Payofski or Paley, was this. A man's dignity is fragile, and in a gutter of a city to the east, Allston's was in pieces.

As the house slept that night Crowell ghosted from room to room. The geometry of lights that fell through the windows on the snow vanished behind him as he drew the draperies. The only lights burned under the pool in the atrium where Mr. Fournier put his seal to affidavits recommending that Allston Lloyd Weir be declared legally insane.

Weir sat up alone, reading, knowing that all he had forgotten lay in wait for him now in his study. It would be there that his memory would sleep. He read under the lamp in the gold room and sometimes a cold breeze turned the page. The woods beyond the river were deep and malign. The endless stream turned the millwheel. The sparkling snow and starlight seemed alloyed in the light of a cosmic foundry. Lights came from the carriage house and spread in circles behind the maple branches. The mountain's craggy face soared over fastnesses of ice.

When it was faintly light and the atrium and pool were dark, he crossed the bedroom and picked up the tape and went downstairs. The pictures he passed, Kiyonaga and Millet, No dancers and the wings of flaming angels, he passed with no regard. Down the staircase he went. Under foot the flagstones in the hall were ice cold. *Five Squares* hung outside the study, a little room with a south exposure and view of a circular courtyard. The room was large but over the years Weir had built bookcases from floor to ceiling and now all his information loomed over the room like intellectual bricks. A cathedral window with a scarlet glass lozenge high up in the center faced the courtyard.

In the middle of the room his desk stood huge and straining under a cargo of manuscript and the strew of a scholar and letter-writer. On a wheeled table by the desk was an old Olympia typewriter—the machine on which he had drafted the philosophy of *Artifact*. He had built his empire on that chaff-choked platen. He bent now and blew on the escapement and a storm of dust and ashes drifted toward a twenty-volume *History of Ideas* in the shelf. Someone had left the cover off. He sat in the cushioned chair. He leaned back and swiveled in the chair, his arms on its arms, his back straight. Out on the courtyard Vitanne had broken bread. The prints of the birds' feet made a meaningful pattern in the snow. Swiveling back to the desk he pushed aside the papers and wiped the blotter clear with his elbow. Across the room an oxblood leather sofa deepened in the light of the brass lamp that he turned on with a key. He opened the desk drawer and brought out the tape player. He tore the noisome wrapper from Paley's tape and put the tape in the machine. Hissing came up and he leaned back. And then from the realm of the real, Warren Paley spoke.

Hello, Allston. So we're done, are we? I am glad.

Hector was by and it's like he knows it might be all up with me. He tells me about these serigraphs he frames and thinks I could knock off in ten minutes. Times a hundred bucks, he says. I have to keep reminding him that life isn't always some pander to fashion. I know he means well. He's afraid for me. I'm going to miss him, if I'm lucky.

I know also that you mean well. What seems strange to me in the end is that you kept thinking I married your daughter to get a break. I guess you'll never know how wrong you were. I married Julie, Mr. Weir, because I thought I could save her. It never made any sense to me that a man could love his daughter like you, or a daughter her father like her. Too bad it took me so long. I've been a pawn in this thing since Concordia, this romance you two tried to hide God knows how long, no. Neither of you can admit it. You probably never admitted it to yourselves. But it's true and it must cause great suffering to both of you . . .

Paley's voice was coarse, drugged as distant as Bertrand's star. Weir pictured him in the studio half insane, his long face an orbit in the candlelight, performing other rituals of his art as if it were magic. As he spoke Weir stood and went to the *History of Ideas*. Behind Taoism to Transcendentalism was his handgun, and he took it out.

... that I have enough on the insurance she can get some kind of a clean start. All the shit she's put up with from us, she deserves that. Then I wouldn't be surprised if you two reconciled. You and I have been childish, Mr. Weir. The fact that you and Celeste could have children at all made me wonder about this world—whether it was some big joke. You don't love her. She doesn't love you. No other explanation for Julie's ... call it rebellion. [Laughter] Christ, Allston, your daughter at Concordia was like one of those wild animals caught in a trap, and to escape she had to gnaw off her leg. She loved you and she had to hide it. I didn't know why. It was a different love and you were too chickenshit to make it happen. Sometimes she'd get into a state over it, and lately when I mess up, you rush right down here and rekindle it all and send her into a tailspin for weeks. Why'd you do that, Allston—come down here and admire yourself in the peephole of that cage they kept for me at McLean, and then pay for it? Did it make you feel whole? You know she used to stare at your picture ...

The gun was a stainless-steel revolver. Weir stared at it blankly, like a man who could form no opinion about it nor fathom its purpose from its design. And Paley spoke.

thought I would take you up on the offer of the horse. If I could be simple, democratic like you said enough once, we might do business. But what did that get Julie or me?

Weir leaned on his elbows. "Why did you put your horse on the moon, Warren?"

and a painting done that way killed the honesty in my case. Freedom in art, Weir, freedom ... Being free. To commit honesties ...

"You hit my daughter."

everything against me, not just my abilities but my lifestyle, me as a man, my marriage, my rejection of the familiar. You coveted my wife. When I realized, what—three years ago—that everything you did was for her, every gesture to help us, flying down here behind your own wife's back, I knew. I couldn't believe it. You had nothing to do with honesty. You fabricated everything. Julie gnawed at that leg, trying to hide it from me, dreaming

[86] *Payofski's Dyscovery*

about you, frustrated in everything she wanted. And all the time you spent with her you spent negating Warren Paley.

"I wanted you to succeed."

. . . you relished my failure. You waited there in your lap of luxury reminding Julie that no one makes it alone, and if she ever, for any reason, wanted to run back to Vermont you would . . .

"Take her back, yes," Weir punched the pause button. He swiveled in the chair, his temple at his finger, his eyes set on the bread frozen in the courtyard. He had hated Warren Paley. So he could not like what Paley drew. But, as Paley himself, he had discovered the humanity and self-privation in that art. He swiveled back again. The gun was waiting. He opened the desk drawer and took a pen from the tray and paper and pushed the machine aside.

My last will and testament . . . all past wills drawn by Celeste and Albert Fournier superseded herewith. I am quite sane. My estate as follows . . .

He turned on the machine. Paley accused him in a level voice carved out of the diction of surrender and Weir wrote his will in the jagged strokes of disgrace. There was an old cigarette in the desk pencil tray. He took it out nervously, rolled the stale paper under his nose, his eyes set and the robe open on his chest. It would be a fine day. Celeste could have the house. Revenues from *Artifact* and the galleries to Bertrand in trust. Paley's work to New York and Amsterdam with letters of introduction. Even if they numbered only five and they shared an asylum room, the people who liked Warren Paley's work would see it, and Weir swiveled, determined now, shaking and more wayward than any man alive. To think of Payofski now was not to arouse his contempt, but envy of the benighted freedom, envy of the charity for self. He drew out more paper and bowed his head.

Dear Vitanne:
    I am sorry to leave you this way and hope you can forgive me. If you could see that Bertrand gets a new wardrobe that fits him properly I would be deeply indebted to you. He can't be confident in himself if he feels marooned in his clothing. I thank you also for your kindness, your diligence and your gentleness. You may destroy that little note in your boot. You are a beautiful and charming young lady. Please keep Bertrand close to you.

Dear Foster:

Don't take it personally. I got sick of your kind of medicine and have made my choice on my own how to be cured. There is a passage in Proust regarding that but unfortunately I don't remember it. My decision to give up the ghost is mine and does not reflect on your medical skills. You are a weak, invidious man in many ways, Foster. You are to leave my family alone. Your cures are sickening. I suggest you take a vacation. I suggest you take Celeste too. You deserve her.

Dearest Bertrand:

One day you will understand why your father did such a terrible thing. Vitanne will help you. I love you very much and hope you can somehow reserve a place for me in your heart. The pain will pass, Bertrand. Trust that my decision brings me peace. I love you.

Dear Celeste:

He lit the cigarette. His lungs filled and opened the robe. His head lightened. Behind him in the cathedral window, dawn crowned the mountain, reminding him that there was nothing—there had always been nothing—to say to her. "Cordially, Allston," he wrote, and took another leaf of paper. He pressed his eyes closed with his fingertips.

My Dearest Julie,

What we did is not forgivable. There are no words. Loving each other as we did was the murder of us as civilized people. If you would even pretend to be good for the time left to you, you can never look at me again.

I understand why you did what you did and do not blame you. You loved Warren even if you could not give him what he wanted. You avenged his wasted life on me. It was a terrifying lie you told me and I can only grieve that the radius of its destruction had to include you also. That night I behaved like a fool, of course. You made me feel young and necessary, however.

Your Warren was right: My love for you was awry. I looked to you as a disinterested man and waited for you to love me like a disinterested woman. And I had to lead Warren's life. It was not easy being Warren Paley.

I am confident you are not laughing at me now and that you are suffering for what we did. Your brother-in-law has a stake in the outcome of all this too, and I wonder what he will sacrifice. We all go down together in our sin though I can only pray it may remain a secret. You must keep it secret.

Please know that in my eyes you did what was necessary to preserve the memory of a courageous artist and free man. You have been courageous yourself and I wish you long life. I love you. I love you too much.

Burn this.

For one without oneself is nothing. Allston Weir sealed the five envelopes and stacked them on the blotter. He leaned back with the gun, opened the cylinder and ejected the bullets. They were 158-grain lead Federals lying in his palm like oiled eggs. One would be plenty, and he put back all six, clicking, one by one.

In the hope his death might yet have dignity he swiveled around twice, scratching his chin with the barrel and eyeing the walls, the oxblood sofa, the stained glass, the shelves. The thought of the bullet ripping through the door frightened him; someone might be eavesdropping. Nor could he justify ruining any number of books in the name of despair, or for that matter the photographs and pictures. That left the window. Well—he swiveled around—the window could be replaced. He eyed the floor. The thought of Vitanne on her knees on the carpet cleaning up the mess irritated him. Projecting the blast beyond his senses, he shook his head. He sashed the robe tighter and pictured the house overrun by the authorities, and Vitanne scrubbing the blood on her knees. That would not do. So—he rolled his chair back to the window and faced the west wall, exposing his left temple to the court and fountain. Dawn had a toehold of blue light on the horizon. He raised the gun and pressed the muzzle against his right temple. The house was still around him. His blood beat in his throat when he swallowed and his finger caressed the trigger. Closing his eyes he could feel death coming on with a stealth that made him shiver. He would be free of a world that demanded respect for certain laws of behavior. No money could buy it off. The simple freedoms of existence as a man without means could no longer hide him from the need for self-respect. The barrel of the gun felt warm and he thought he heard, across the wasteland of his thoughts, Payofski laughing, holding out his filthy hands through the darkness of a life valued for its lack of responsibility and error.

He squeezed the trigger slowly. With his heart pounding the curl of the metal pressed his finger and the torus of the barrel made a ring in front of his ear. It felt as if the barrel created a vacuum that sucked his temple against the tunnel that would free it by blowing his brains out the window. There was a pressure point of the trigger and he knew—or once knew—where it was. To time his final thought he perceived as his last duty on earth, to leave it incomplete, to carry it away with him to eternity. He did not feel well. It was dark and cold, and he was a murd

"*Pkeieu!*"

"I killed him—the wolf taurent, Father! There! At the window!"

Allston slid the gun into his lap and stared hopelessly. Bertrand stood in the doorway in his briefs. There was a mist of tears in his eyes. His hair was scattered every which way.

"What taurent," Allston was hoarse. He tried to clear it with gruff. "What are you doing up this late?"

The boy padded across the room and peered over the chaotic desk.

"Go wake Vitanne, Bertrand. Have her make your breakfast."

"Vitanne went," said Bert.

"What do you mean, she went?"

"Mummy said. Last night she said. You're fired!"

Allston turned inward and bent harried over the desk. "When?"

"In the kitchen. Mummy said yes, that means. And Vitanne said she said Good! You're a horrible bitch! So Mummy slapped her. Like this!" Mightily Bertrand wound up with his left hand and slapped himself. His feet came off the floor, his body twisted in midair, he made the face of a ghoul. He crashed to the floor and rolled against the bookcase where some photographs on the top shelf splattered down on his belly. He twitched—and he was dead. "Bertrand," Weir rubbed his head. "You're ruining everything."

The boy revived and sat up Indian fashion and eyed his distraught father. He picked up the photographs and played with them. "Vitanne kissed me before she went. Here is Vitanne," he said, "and Mummy and here is Dr. Ames bear on taurent skill of Procyon. Julie before I came. And here graduated."

"Bring them here."

The boy brought them around. Allston took them away. In the top picture she was nineteen or twenty and Allston stared, horrified. She was beautiful even then; the darkness of her secret had no hold on her eyes. Arrested, the pistol in his lap, Allston saw her dressed in white robes and a mortarboard in the shade of a willow tree. . . . I think it must have been then that he felt the kick in his heart, the second he looked hard, bringing the picture up to his face. He did not remember the ceremony, but something . . . Julie standing there, turned that way. (I do remember it. I was in the picture beside Julie when it was taken.) There was a barbecue—kebab and burnt peppers, mint tea, raspberry chocolate cake. Julie had turned in the direction of a car that backfired, and I had turned to look at the same thing. When I first saw the picture I wanted it destroyed for

Allston's sake. I wanted the head of the man who didn't keep his car in tune and I made a mental note to tear it up, and the negative too, if not to keep out of sight of the one who had taken the picture, who must have seen within the frame exactly what the picture would mean to us. But I didn't destroy it. And that morning Weir held it so close, his eyes pinched. His heart pounded even harder. He seemed to know exactly what we were looking at, if not to remember the day perfectly. He blinked and a sound came out of him, "Ahh," softly.

Bertrand looked up at his father's eyes. Weir held the picture close and when he looked at Bert, he smiled. He turned his eyes up to the ceiling, the photo pressed to his breast, his eyes shut. "Ah, God," he said.

"Father?"

". . . God, Jesus Christ!"

"Father?"

Weir looked at the boy. The epiphanies of the ring that had freed him from the Washington Street Shelter for Wayward Men, the news from Maurice that his scans were negative, paled in the grip of this picture.

"Bertrand," he whispered. "Where is your mother?"

"Asleep."

"Where? Asleep in what room?"

"The blue room. She puts stuff in her hands, squish. Squish and wears eyelashes to bed."

"Eyel . . ." Allston looked back at the photograph, held it with his eyes lovingly, and lowered it.

"I want you to go to the kitchen," he said, "and make your breakfast, Bert. Then go to the atrium and tell Mr. Fournier I would like him to meet me in the blue room. Tell him to bring my will. Can you remember that?"

Bertrand screwed up his forehead.

"And put on some warm clothes," Weir said. "We're going for a ride."

"Where!" Bertrand jumped up.

"To Boston. Do as I say. Hurry."

Allston pushed away from his desk, hitched his bathrobe sash tight, tore up the five letters and went upstairs for his trousers. He came back down with a fixed smile and set out for the blue room, still with his robe on. At the door of the blue room he did not knock. He pushed it open and shadowed it, tall and smiling. His gun hung loose at his side like the key to the door. He didn't need it. I had seen that smile when we played chess and the game was hopelessly in his favor.

But he said, "Good morning, Ames—Celeste?" And I lifted my head from Celeste's breast. He came in ahead of the light, grinning. Stunned, Celeste got up on her elbows.

"Allston?"

"Forgive me. Did I wake you?"

"Allston?"

"Ames, if you would get out of bed and collect yourself. We're going for a ride, you and I."

"Allston . . ."

"That's my name," he said. "I've had no relapse that I remember, and I'm quite aware of what I'm doing. Now who was it said that?" he lowered his chin in a cup of his fingers and thought. He was unshaven and depressed. "Ah, Warren Paley." He flourished the gun, smiled his smile and waved the barrel in a sine including Celeste. "Dress, Ames."

I pushed the sheets back and got out of bed. Odd, being naked in front of him. I was going to ask him if I could explain, when Bertrand came through the door swallowing a mouthful of cereal and milk to announce that Mr. Fournier was coming. And then I saw that Ally had the photograph in his hand.

"Tell him to bring his hat and coat, Bertrand," Weir said, and the boy bolted again.

"Allston?" Celeste drew the sheet over her. "It's not what it seems. If you want some confession . . ."

"I do, but not now, and not yours. Dress, Foster. Stat, damn you."

"Where are we going?"

"Boston. It's a town in Massachusetts."

"I think we can do without the gun, Ally."

"No, I like how it feels," he smiled. "I'll like how it jumps too if you get clever with me. The stakes are high today. Your opinion of me as a man too sick to lead his own life will be the end for you unless you do what I say, starting now. I never judged your impositions with my wife, I would thank you not to judge my choice of weapon. You have it cushy," he put his hand in his pocket and stepped into the room. "Sleeping in my house and eating from my pantry, drinking my liquor, signing your own paychecks and diddling my wife. Now I may have a sick memory, but it's clear to me that there's nothing here worth the wait to advance my happiness. Nothing except this," and he held the picture up, bent concave in his hand.

"Allston, you're not well."

"Exactly. And I've got a gun. Dress."

I was doing that when Fournier rounded the corner, lost with his hat and coat over his arm. He had a little diskette on his thumb and an expression of great uneasiness. His breast pocket sagged under the ink pens and his vest was stained with runaway red ink and smoked salmon. A man who could amortize this and arbitrage that, he was a lawyer and accountant, one felt, looking at him, whether he liked it or not. He came in and stared a moment, cleared his throat and quickly tried to leave.

"Mr. Fournier," Weir said. "Have you finished the will you were drawing?"

Fournier glanced at the handgun. "No, sir," he stammered. "That would be around seven a.m. Per my contract with Mrs. Weir."

"That disk in your hand. Is that the will as it stands so far? The revised version? The only draft?"

"Yes sir."

"Put it in your coat pocket, Mr. Fournier."

Fournier fidgeted. "Perhaps if I had till six, sir . . ."

"Just put the disk in your coat, Mr. Fournier, and put your coat on. Do it now."

Not that a large gun in the hands of a man represented to Mr. Fournier as legally insane justified any debate, but Fournier had no spine, in my opinion. He stood there like erect mush regretting, if the result was to be murder, his allegiance to the woman of the house. He put the disk in his coat, however. Allston lifted the gun as if the power pleased him. He said, "Hurry up, Foster."

"Allston!" Celeste shouted. "What are you doing with that disk!"

"Why just now leaving with it, darling," he smiled. "You will of course not call the police? Now, Mr. Fournier? Onward? Ames?"

My car was in the drive—1956 T-bird, a peridot chartreuse with white interior, a convertible. It had wire spoke wheels and fat whitewalls. A nice car. When everybody piled in—Bertrand in the front, Weir behind Bertrand and Fournier behind me—I heard her groan. Bertrand asked if we could put the top down and Weir said, "Yes," and I had to put the goddamn top down. I don't think it was forty out but we were off to Boston.

We roared away under the sun, north to the highway. Bertrand with his maple gun distracted me more than Allston with his cannon. The boy wore a coat about five times too big; it had a fur-lined hood, his head in there so deep you couldn't see his face, only the torquing hood to give an indication he was among us. He shot at everything we passed—wolfcrows and what-have-you—unfortunately no police. He had too much imagination for his own good. It would be useless trying to apply real names to these things he shot at, whether A-frames on Route 9 or when we climbed, the sun-jeweled mountains, that chained tiara of the horizon, winter rock sheathed in ice on ledges over the road. We shot past sugar houses and the woods and Weir said, "Drive faster, Ames." I drove faster. Fournier's teeth chattered calculations of chance to keep a step ahead of his fear—Route 9 for one hour, Route 2 at 760 feet, a declivity of sm900 feet, 95 for 28 minutes, ft/second squared if I miss this hairpin. He held his hat down and appeared to be crying but it was only tears from the slipstream. A deep S-curve pressed Bertrand against the stickshift, which he shot. His body jerked around in that big immobile coat. Deep in the hood he spat out *pkiieue*s and threats, the sound of rockets leveled against everything wolfish or contradictory. He was in his element. I was freezing.

"Procyon phraxtuns at seven thousand feet, Father!" he screamed over the back and blasted away as his father stared at me. Little pieces of cereal flecked the windshield and on we flew, a whispering swish past the sleeping houses and the farms. At some point in the first two hours it occurred to me that Allston was dying. It was something in his look— the stare in the mirror half sick, half loving, as if he had finally figured it all out and who, really, could I blame but myself? I felt that my only hope of staying alive in the face of his anger would be if fate sent down another relapse. If that happened he would get the stunned look, he would get dizzy and forget where he was and why he was armed. The picture in his hand would make no sense to him, the boy, the top down in autumn, the time of day, the car, this nation and my name, the absurd attitude of the accountant would all be the deepest mysteries to him.

I drove as if trying to escape from him. We soared by woods, factories and jerkwater towns knotted around a post office. The whitewalls sang on the pavement and the snow melted. Celeste did not call the police— no. If she called the police Allston would fling the disk into oblivion and double Fournier's salary to vouch for his competence. Weir engaged Mr. Fournier in some shouted conversation about painting but it was clear he was only reassuring the lawyer or trying to gauge his depth. Every now and then Allston would pull out the snapshot and look at it and fix me in the mirror with a look that oscillated between glower and sorrow. The picture—I had let it exist as a confession to him at the time, and I hadn't even known it.

But when I guessed that and even made peace with myself—with those elements of me that are closed to me and open to everyone but me— we were barreling down Route 2. As we crested the hill and soared down, Boston broached the sky. Beside me Bertrand woke from a nap and started another oneiric firefight. He trained his gun on Belmont, site of the mental hospital that rang with Warren Paley's screams and laughter for ten years. Behind me Fournier sat holding his hat down and Weir's eyelids drooped. We went around some traffic circles, down an avenue with laboratories and a tree-lined street with an observatory. Densely populated. Now Bertrand merely looked around as if he thought we were on Procyon at last. He shivered and fingered the deed, rubbernecking in the big hood at the Garden Street firehouse, then the gold-leaf sign of the Capital of the Age of Enlightenment. He aimed his gun at it but fell silent and held his fire. Weir said, "Parallel the river, Ames. Go east," and we did. Till there was no more east and we arched a ramp over the river and closed it down in a spiraling maze of steel and concrete. "Foster!" Weir yelled. His head was cocked in the mirror. His hair blew back wild. I think I would have traded my license to practice for a stiff drink.

"We each have a lie," he yelled, "for everybody we meet, and the wish to live it out. Sound familiar?"

I nodded.

He clenched his jaw. "Well I want you to know that I know what your lie was for us. Now zip up my son and take a right!"

So we stamped up the wood stairs of the old winery where his daughter lived—the same stairs Hector Paley had pistol-whipped him down and that he now herded me up with a piece of his own. At the landing he knocked and stared at me. A long time passed before we heard Julie. Her footsteps came, the door opened a crack and she peered out. When she freed up the chain Bertrand ran into her arms. Fournier, Weir and I followed him in.

She bent down and hugged her brother; there was a lot of fuss and mumbling, understanding nods, confusion and tears. "Good to see you,

Julie," I said. "You look well," and sat at the table overlooking the garden. Pregnancy had not changed her much. She looked as self-absorbed and beautiful as always. As she held Bertrand's face under hers she laughed and kissed him deep in the hood.

"Daddy?" she turned to Weir. "Who is he, and why are you pointing a gun at him?"

"Mr. Fournier," Weir said, "give me that disk, please." Fournier did. Weir took some kitchen shears from a drawer and cut the disk in half. Returning the halves to Fournier he pulled out his wallet and gave the frazzled man a twenty. "Bus fare home," he said, "and here"—one hundred—"severance pay. You're fired, Mr. Fournier."

"Of course I am, sir. Thank you." Fournier hastened out as if escaping with his life.

"Bertrand," Weir said. "Go into the studio and look at the paintings."

"I want to see Julie."

"Bert."

He stared at me, then went away. The sounds of war erupted in Paley's studio but it was followed by a curious silence. I was interested myself in seeing what Paley had left the world; there's a morbid curiosity attached to the work of a dead man, and certainly Warren, alive, had been different from us. I might even have bid on one if I had had the time. But Julie turned to her father, I think dying to explain herself. "Daddy, I want you to know . . . "

"Not now."

"What Hector did, I told him . . . "

"It's all right."

"I tried . . . "

"Be quiet, Julie."

"I was alone."

"Ames," said Weir, "there's bourbon in the cupboard. Pour two drinks."

I stood and Julie stepped away from me. I got the glasses, the bottle and the ice. It didn't matter that it was nine in the morning, I poured two big tumblers and sipped my bourbon and Allston sipped his and stared, relishing what he had learned. I looked down at the alley where Paley had looked down, and where Weir had looked down as Paley, as I would learn later, and Paley and Weir both looked down as wayward men.

"Do you know," Weir sipped his drink, "who the father of this baby is, Ames?" He put his hand on Julie's belly.

"At the landfill you suggested you were."

"And would you say, Ames, that it's too late to abort this baby?"

"Morally I wouldn't say. Biologically, no."

Julie looked away.

"I don't give a damn for your morals," Weir said. "What would you say this baby's chances are of being born whole. With a good mind. With all its faculties."

"Very good."

"What?"

"Its chances. Of being born normal are very good." I sipped my drink. He looked at Julie.

"Julie," he said. "Will you marry me?"

"Oh, Daddy."

"Allston . . . ," I said.

"Did you ever think about marrying Celeste, Ames? Seriously. I'd give her to you, you know."

"You're very kind."

"She'll be my mother-in-law," he smiled.

"Of course . . . "

"Julie is my lover."

"If that's your choice," I said, "I wish you the best."

He glared at me and turned to Julie and said, "There's been a mistake, Julie. We are not entirely to blame. Do you understand?"

"Yes."

"You do?"

She nodded, "When I was twenty. There's a picture in your study in . . . "

"Yes, yes," Weir turned to me. "Ames, say it for me. Say it aloud. She's a fine young lady, considering her upbringing. I did well by her, didn't I? Didn't I? The diapers? The braces?"

"Yes, you did well."

"Then say it. The truth. Tell the truth. Think of your reputation, what's left of it."

I looked down at the garden, then at Allston. I stood and put my hands in my pockets. Julie was staring at me.

"Allston," I said. "You're not Julie's father. I am."

Payofski's Dyscovery [97]

Julie took Allston's arm as they walked along the channel ahead of Bert and me that day. As it was the day Warren Paley died, Allston had stopped in Boston on his way to California because Warren had begged him. Paley was just out of the hospital and Julie said he had planned everything—the lunch meeting, the slides he wanted to show, to explain, notes on responses to objections, all fiercely logical. When Weir was ushered to the table in the restaurant on the thirty-ninth floor, Paley was chain smoking. In a bad way, nervous and numb from medication, he spilled coffee as the slides went through Weir's fingers. Weir studied them and sipped his drink and glanced at the bruised cheek Julie kept turned to the window . . .

When he put the slides down he folded his hands and looked at Paley. He looked at Julie and cleared his throat, and looked at the tablecloth and said that he regretted it, but he still had the same problem with these pictures. Nothing had changed. He spoke in a level voice saying he thought they failed their intention and that Warren had not done with his subject matter what he should have. He was going the wrong way with his technique; he was not painting what people were buying. He could not break the rules like that, the buying public would break him.

Julie coughed and glared at her father. As she looked out at the sky a jet a mile away lifted its nose above the level of the thirty-eighth floor. Paley sat hunched, his face grayish white, twirling his cigarette ash in thought and when he finally spoke, he was incoherent. He began rambling. His eyes tripped over the table, the glasses and the slides. Politely Allston said he had a plane to catch, and he pulled out his wallet to pay. But Paley grabbed it.

"Look again. Please, Allston," he said. "You missed it. Look here. Do you see? Can't you see? *See!*" People at other tables turned to see. Allston held his head and shut his eyes. The lights that came before an episode of his illness winked on and off in his head. Bending to the table he said, "Look." He could not think what the painter's name was. "There's no place in *Artifact* for these. Believe me. There's no place in this *epoch* for these. Trust me . . . Look, what you can do—what I . . ." he turned his hand over and leaned in, "what I'd like you to do is sell them to me. And I'll keep them for you."

Paley stared.

"I'll buy them," Allston said. "I'll give you twenty thousand for these three. I'll . . . keep them. Maybe one day . . . "

Paley stared at him. "What."

"What?" Allston pinched his eyes shut with his fingers. "You want to sell them, don't you? You want money?"

Paley stared at the tablecloth. When he looked up his eyes were ablaze, his mouth was still; his face was drawn. "One day," he whispered, "what."

Allston glanced helplessly at Julie and stood, folding his napkin. "I don't know what he wants and apparently he doesn't either." Paley stood too. It was clear to any number of people in the room that there was a man who had broken through. Julie followed him and her father to the lobby where the maitre d' stepped between the men, the benefactor and the painter. Paley was trying to grab Weir's arm. Maybe he didn't remember he had the wallet and by then Allston didn't remember either. He turned and looked at the man with the long hair staring at him. Who was he? Warren backed away, up the stairs leading to the observation deck, murmuring, "One day," shaking his head, "tomorrow," his smile was stuck, "Take the money, Warren," a strange smile. Allston, his head spinning, leaned into the elevator. Frozen by her father's offer Julie called to Warren on the stairs, then called to her father as the elevator doors closed. And down he went to the oblivion on the street. He didn't know which way to turn. He started walking. When Julie came down in another elevator and stepped out, glancing up and down the crowded street, she saw her father seated, and Warren . . .

People were running up to him. They made a circle, a ring of faces, elbowing each other. The sidewalk was cracked under the body of a noon-time celebrity. The traffic lurched and seized up at the blood of a shattered man.

A cold wind blew trash and paper against a bollard on the channel where Bert and I waited. I remember gazing at our images in the thick water and Bertrand asking me why Julie was crying and why I, a doctor, didn't give her some medicine. I don't remember feeling overly guilty, really, though I was certainly relieved. I became less intimately bound with Allston's life, and with respect to the past we shared, as to how it would manifest itself in my private future, you will understand I was on my own. . . .

In February Celeste moved to New York City. Vitanne Geneau was invited to continue studying at Concordia but she declined and lives in

London now. With the help of a gift from Allston, Maurice Topsenfeld set up two clinics in the city which operate on a system of barter.

Allston kept me on with the understanding that it was because I am the leading authority on his illness, but he was to be the leading authority on his life. He asked me to do him a favor and said he would not take no for an answer. On April first in Vermont, Julie took my arm on the balcony and looked downstairs through a veil at the people who glared upstairs at her. Crowell nodded, and Bertrand raised the velvet pillow and descended and turned at the newel and bore the ring under the eyes of Reverend Elvin Gaus in the library. Smoke from Dr. Topsenfeld's cigar flumed the light in the oriel, which silvered Allston's hair and purpled the vestment. The reverend's voice echoed hushed vows, and the vows' hush echoed, Bertrand watched his father and sister's lips crease the sunlight. Their lips touched, and in the delirium the people shut their eyes, and when they opened them Julie bowed her head to Allston's shoulder. Allston bowed his head and touched the ends of her hair. Closing the book, Reverend Gaus said, "I pronounce you husband and wife," and under his breath he said, *Heaven help us*, and in their stares, the people, *Heaven help us*. Mr. Richfield, half sober, his boutonniere going up and down like a flame, launched into Mozart's *Fantasia* in C minor on the Steinway and the room tinkled and shimmered. Conversation halted, then flowed. The champagne hissed in the crystal like the sea.

Twenty-six of Warren's paintings and drawings toured three American cities last year. Hector, shock-paroled by the Governor of Massachusetts, managed the exhibit. The critics responded to the show with a certain bewildered vehemence, but the painters, all stained nails and apprehensive eyes, met in the bars and drank doubles to Paley. The show is losing less and less money.

A month before her wedding Julie gave birth to a boy—seven pounds ten ounces. The blood test demanded by Celeste's attorneys confirmed what Julie and Allston knew by the infant's brooding look and the way he claimed her breast—that his father was Warren Paley. He is named Warren too, though he is too small to know it yet, or to care.